MURDER
AT
BUCKINGHAM PALACE

Murder
at
Buckingham Palace

T.E.B. Clarke

St. Martin's Press
New York

Author's note

The author would like it to be known that staff conditions at Buckingham Palace today are very different from those prevailing in the 1930s. Royal servants now have their own union, a guarantee that they are adequately paid, work limited hours and receive all reasonable amenities. In those days the running of Britain's premier residence was largely in the hands of persons who, while perhaps not consciously uncaring, were brought up to be indifferent to the needs and struggles of their social inferiors.

Elegant living may be a thing of the past, but regret at its going must be tempered with thought of its harshness for the many.

MURDER AT BUCKINGHAM PALACE. Copyright © 1981 by T.E.B. Clarke.
All rights reserved. Printed in the United States of America.
No part of this book may be used or reproduced in any manner
whatsoever without written permission except in the case of brief
quotations embodied in critical articles or reviews. For information,
address St. Martin's Press, 175 Fifth Avenue, New York, N.Y. 10010.

Library of Congress Cataloging in Publication Data

Clarke, Thomas Ernest Bennett, 1907-
    Murder at Buckingham Palace.

    I. Title.
PR6005.L453M8   1982   823'.912   81-16739
ISBN 0-312-55282-3   AACR2

Foreword

When death occurs within the precincts of a Royal residence it becomes the duty of the King's (or Queen's) Coroner to hold an inquest in either that or another Royal building. Happily, there has seldom been a need for his services: the records show that holders of the office have dealt with only seven cases during the present century.

An eighth case has however been omitted from those records. There is no mention of an inquest conducted in strict secrecy at St James's Palace in the early summer of 1935. Nearly all of those involved in the affair are now dead, and it would almost certainly have been lost without trace in Court history but for the recent finding of a private record kept by Ex-Detective Chief Inspector Harry Bennett, late of Scotland Yard.

Harry Bennett died in 1979 at the age of 72. He had talked freely of the many cases he handled in his distinguished career, yet never of the events on which this narrative version of his record is based and in which Harry Bennett played a principal part, though at the time holding the modest rank of detective sergeant: a murder in, of all places, Buckingham Palace—and, of all times, only a few days before the Silver Jubilee of King George V and Queen Mary.

It is not easy to condone a cover-up in high places; but there are occasions when circumstances demand it for the public good. This surely was one of them; for news that a murderer was at large in Their Majesties' London home would undoubtedly have cast a fearsome shadow over that week of national rejoicing.

1

"Nothing is to disturb me short of H.M.'s death."

Chief Inspector Robert Botterell recalled his last words to his deputy as his brother-in-law's voice broke in on a dream already fading.

"You're wanted on the phone, Bob. It's the Palace." Jack Sinnott was at the bedroom door in his pyjamas.

"What's the time?" Botterell reached for his watch as he swung his legs out of bed, awake with the immediacy of the experienced police officer.

"Just gone half past seven. I hate to wake you, Betty and I were saying how tired you looked, but your man there insisted it's urgent."

So it must be, Botterell reflected as he hurried downstairs to the only telephone in the Sinnotts' modest Clapham house. A bachelor in his forty-second year, Botterell had rooms in the south-west corner of Buckingham Palace, where he was deputy chief of the two dozen men from 'A' Division of the Metropolitan Police assigned to Palace duties. Occasionally, as now, he accepted a standing invitation to spend a leave day and night at the home of his married sister. Today, Wednesday the 1st of May 1935 he had greater cause than usual to welcome the break. The Silver Jubilee of King George V and Queen Mary was to be celebrated on Monday of next week, and the past month had entailed a load of extra work to ensure against any slip-up on the great day. The strain upon him had been at once apparent to Betty and Jack, and Botterell was sure that Inspector Calkin, left in charge of the Palace section, must be equally aware of his need for a long sleep and a day of complete relaxation; he had in fact mentioned he was planning to take his young nephew and niece this afternoon to the new zoo at Whipsnade. Charles Calkin was an efficient and confident policeman who could be relied on to handle any ordinary emergency with unflurried competence. Only a major crisis could put him on the phone to his superior officer at this hour on a leave day.

"Nothing short of His Majesty's death . . . " Pray God not at this of all times!

Botterell picked up the receiver from the hall table. "What is it, Charlie?"

"I think you ought to come, sir. There's been an accident."

"In the Royal Family?"

"No, no, nothing like that—they're still at Windsor. It's here in the Palace. A girl has died."

"What girl? How?"

"One of the housemaids. It looks like a fall off a ladder. A book ladder in the Old Library. She might have been using it for dusting along a high shelf."

Sympathy came a bad third to relief and vexation. "Poor girl. But why the hell wake me up at a time like this, Calkin? A fatal accident to a junior servant. Very sad and all that, but surely to God it's something you can cope with?"

"I daresay I could, sir; but a death in the Palace—I thought it only right for you to be informed, seeing that Superintendent Gardner isn't due back from Windsor till later this morning."

"Lucky for you, my lad! He'd have roasted you alive."

Superintendent Sidney Gardner was the King's bodyguard. An officer of the uniformed branch though himself never seen in uniform, he was chief of the Palace police but, unlike Botterell, travelled always with H.M.

"Bad enough getting me out of bed," Botterell grumbled on. "Why in God's name you think the Super would be interested—"

Calkin said almost casually: "Only because it seems to have been the same kind of accident that Lily Farrow had, if you remember that incident."

Botterell stiffened. "I'll come."

He certainly did remember that 'incident'. He and Calkin had worked on it together in the days before they had joined the Royal Household. Lily Farrow was a prostitute whose body had been found in an empty house in Horseferry Road. No connection with any ladder—Inspector Calkin was being commendably discreet. Lily Farrow had been clubbed to death.

2

Of all the six hundred-odd rooms in Buckingham Palace few if any were less used than the Old Library on the north-east side of the inner quadrangle.

Over the years it had been the conceit of certain authors and publishers to have copies of their books impressively bound for presentation to the reigning sovereign. It was doubtful whether that personage had opened more than one in a hundred of these unsolicited offerings. Sir Charles Cust, equerry to King George V, once described them to His Majesty as "beautifully bound piffle". The King subsequently gave orders for the piffle to be ruthlessly weeded out.

The destruction of such handsome volumes would have been vandalism; passing them on to a dealer would have risked the indignation and hurt feelings of an observant donor; it was therefore decided to fix extra shelves for these unwanted and mostly unreadable works in what had long ago been the private library of the Prince Consort, itself already a bibliographical mausoleum.

Nowadays the Old Library was confined to occasional use as an overflow room for anyone whose office was being renovated. At other times almost its only visitors were the housemaids detailed to keep the room free of dust, and their immediate superior, the head housemaid—ever watchful for evidence of slackness among the female staff under her command.

It was however the latter's own superior who had this morning found the dead girl. Mrs Wells, assistant housekeeper, was a tall, dark, sharp-faced woman with a quiet, precise voice, who performed her duties without fuss and rarely showed any semblance of a smile. Chief Inspector Botterell, knocking at the locked door of the library some twenty minutes after receiving

Calkin's summons, was admitted to find her closeted alone with his deputy.

Botterell's eyes went past them to the small still figure on the faded blue carpet. "Where's the doctor?"

"Been and gone," Calkin said. "He'll be back as soon as he's dressed. Nothing he could do for her. He estimates she's been dead at least ten hours."

Botterell moved closer to the victim whose name he was later to learn. Alice Gill, aged 20, seven months in Royal service. A slim but full-breasted girl, with well-shaped legs in black cotton stockings as far as they could be seen below the skirt of the pale blue housemaid's uniform. She lay on her back, face turned up towards the high ceiling. In life a pretty girl, Botterell guessed, though far from pretty now: blood-streaked white cap awry on light brown bobbed hair matted with dried blood; at least three ugly contusions separately visible on temple and upper forehead. There was no doubt whatever that she had been done to death by repeated heavy blows from the all-too-familiar blunt instrument.

Botterell looked around the room which he was seeing for the first time. Not a large room by Palace standards, maybe thirty feet by twenty: eight shelves of books, mostly in tooled leather, covering all available wall space to a foot beneath the ceiling; an oak table of massive design bearing only a blotter of surely the largest size made. Behind it was a high-backed chair close to the tall first-floor windows; dark blue velvet curtains were only half drawn back, though widely enough for the bright morning sun to spotlight the sad little fallen figure. Two leather armchairs, an oak stool, a rectangular side table with a telephone on it. And the book ladder of which Calkin had spoken: a fixed stepladder with holding post, topped by a square platform on which the browser might rest a volume too weighty to be easily brought down.

At least six feet separated the base of the ladder from the nearest point of the body. Calkin spoke as Botterell was gazing reflectively from one to the other. "You can say what you're thinking, sir. Mrs Wells is under no illusion."

"She'd have had to fall off that thing several times to get those injuries," Mrs Wells said. "And she wouldn't have been lying on her back, would she?"

"You didn't touch the body?"

"Only to see if the girl was still breathing. I knew then she had been dead for some hours." She added, as if to allay misgiving and perhaps explain her coolness, "I was a V.A.D. in the war."

"I see. Tell me, would the girl have had cause to visit this room last night?"

"Yes, to draw the curtains. That always has to be done, one never knows who may decide to use the room. Not that many ever do."

"But she wouldn't have been dusting at that hour?"

"Without a duster? I think not."

Botterell could have kicked himself for the oversight. Not that he'd ever considered himself a detective. He turned back to Calkin. "The doctor of course realizes how she died?"

The Inspector nodded. "He's as anxious as I've been to make sure it doesn't get out."

A gentle knock at the door and the doctor was back in person to confirm that. "My God, what a hell of a thing to happen here!" Third in rank of the resident medical staff, Dr Roger Flint was an ebullient man of reddish colouring, his smooth round face and thick curly hair outwardly taking a few years off his age of 43. He eyed Botterell. "This makes four of us in the know. You've told nobody else, Chief Inspector?"

"No one so far, Doctor. Superintendent Gardner will have to know of course, and so will the Palace Steward—I'll leave it to him to inform the Master of the Household." He turned again to the assistant housekeeper. "I gather you, Mrs Wells, have not left this room since you made the discovery?"

She shook her head. "I asked for Superintendent Gardner on the telephone here. That was stupid of me—I think it was the shock—I should have remembered he would still be at Windsor Castle with Their Majesties. When the girl told me there was no reply I had myself put through to your office. Inspector Calkin answered. I told him there had been an accident, that was all. He asked me to stay where I was and admit nobody else till he arrived."

Botterell nodded approval. His deputy and pupil, twelve years his junior, had clearly handled this supreme test impeccably, endorsing his oft-expressed view that Charlie Calkin was destined to go far in the job.*

Calkin was saying to Mrs Wells, "Please repeat exactly what you told me about finding the girl."

She addressed Botterell, propriety now and then awarding the doctor a fleeting glance. "At ten minutes past seven Lady Ruxford's maid telephoned me to complain that the grate had not been cleared or the fire laid and lit in her ladyship's sitting-room."

"Two of the Ladies-in-Waiting have apartments in this corridor," Calkin reminded his chief.

"I spoke at once to Ellen Carter, the head housemaid for this floor, and I was told by her that Alice Gill was the housemaid responsible. Carter said she would send Gill up as soon as she could find her.

"I then visited the rooms of Lady Wittlesham to see whether the girl had also neglected the grate in there. I found this was so. Her ladyship was asleep and I didn't want to risk disturbing her by using the telephone in there to speak to Carter again. The nearest other telephone was here in the Old Library, so I came in here to use it and that was when I saw Gill."

"So you didn't speak to Ellen Carter that second time."

"No. I expect she has been looking for me to report Gill missing. I hope she has had the good sense to send somebody else to the Ladies' apartments."

"She has," Dr Flint said. "I passed a couple of housemaids on my way here."

"They didn't see you enter the library?" This sharply from Botterell.

"Not unless one turned round and came back."

"But seeing the doctor about at this hour will tell them something's happened," Calkin observed.

"The accident story will naturally have to come out soon," Botterell said. He turned back to the doctor. "I believe you think she was killed last night?"

"It's difficult to say without a proper examination, but the present stage of *rigor mortis* suggests she has been lying here for

*Chief Inspector Botterell was right. Charles Calkin retired in 1961 as Assistant Commissioner.

the best part of twelve hours."

"Does each girl have a room of her own, Mrs Wells?"

"Good gracious, no." He might have asked the question in a house with a mere dozen bedrooms rather than several hundred. "All the lower servants share. She would have either one or two companions, that is something I shall have to ascertain."

"Yet as far as you know they didn't report her absence last night."

"Quite. But that wouldn't altogether surprise me. These girls stick together, one wouldn't want to get another into trouble."

Botterell added import to his tone. "Now think carefully, Mrs Wells. Can you be absolutely certain that nobody saw you enter this room?"

She hardly needed to pause. "There was nobody about. And if I had heard footsteps I am sure I'd have looked round to see if it was Gill arriving late."

"That's good. Now, Mrs Wells, I'm going to ask you to do something that isn't easy. I want you to leave this room now, making sure nobody sees you come out, and then wipe the last half-hour completely out of your mind. You haven't seen Alice Gill, you know nothing except that Ellen Carter hasn't been able to find her this morning. Will you take it from there, act as you normally would if a housemaid is reported missing?"

"I can do that," she said. A slight frown. "I shall have to report the matter of course to Mrs Percival"—she was referring to the Palace housekeeper—"and I hope she never learns I knew more than I told her."

"I hope so too," Botterell said with feeling. "But if the worst should happen I assure you I shall see to it that you won't suffer. You are acting under my strict orders."

Mrs Wells made her cautious departure with as near an expression of satisfaction as her sombre face would permit itself. The junior of the two assistants, she had resigned herself to the near-certain promotion of Mrs Holloway to the coveted post of housekeeper when Mrs Percival retired in two years' time. Now surely she, Florence Wells, could hope for a reversal of the situation. Could they possibly be so unfair as to pass her over if she acquitted herself without flaw in a crisis of this magnitude? She warmed to Alice Gill in death as never in life. She had not known the girl at all well but disapproved of what she had seen of her. A fast little piece and saucy with it. And undeniably pretty. Miss Florence Wells—no self-respecting housekeeper would let herself be known as anything but 'Mrs'—was not one to appreciate pretty girls.

"I think we'll be lucky in that one," Inspector Calkin said as the carefully opened door closed behind her. "Most women couldn't get out fast enough to spread it abroad."

"She'll have to open up at the inquest," Flint pointed out.

Botterell shrugged. "By then it'll be out of our hands. In fact I'm going to set about passing the buck right now. The three of us will leave here separately, first making doubly sure the coast is clear. I'll go out last and lock this door behind me. I suggest, Doctor, you and Inspector Calkin explain matters to the Palace Steward while I go personally to Scotland Yard."

"Taking it straight to the Commissioner?" Calkin queried.

Botterell nodded. "If ever there was top priority, this is it. A killer on the loose in Buck House—we've got to nail the bastard and quick!" He looked down again at the little sprawled figure, conscience suddenly stirred by the realization of how cursorily they had dwelt on her tragedy. "Poor kid. Little did she dream how close she'd come to causing a world sensation."

3

"So she hasn't yet been found—is that what you're suggesting?"

There was a touch of incredulity in the Commissioner's voice. Still reeling somewhat from the enormity of it all, the Commissioner was only gradually adapting himself to the necessity for a murder investigation to be conducted in a manner surely without precedent.

In the '30s the office of Commissioner of the Metropolitan Police was still the perquisite of retired Army officers; the present incumbent had not held it long enough to be as invulnerable to shock as the seasoned policeman. Summoned early from his Westminster home on a matter of extreme urgency, he had found Chief Inspector Botterell awaiting him at Scotland Yard some fifteen minutes later. They were joined shortly afterwards by Sir Wilfred Jennings, Master of the King's Household.

Also present now in the Commissioner's office were the Assistant Commissioner who was head of the Criminal Investigation Department and Deputy Commander William Roe, chief of the Special Branch, whose responsibilities were headed by arrangements for the protection of the highest in the land.

It was Botterell who was being addressed but it was Roe who answered the Commissioner. "I think, sir, that's the right procedure."

"Assuming the woman can be trusted to play her part."

"I am quite sure Mrs Wells won't let us down," Sir Wilfred said with conviction.

"If she's not reliable," the A.C. observed calmly, "the damage will have been done already, so we shan't be risking much there."

A nod of circumspect agreement. "Very well. Let's get it over as soon as possible. This woman—Mrs Wells—has been told the girl is missing. She questions the maid who shares a room with her, gets it out of the girl that this other girl—the dead one, what was her name?"

"Alice Gill," Botterell prompted.

"She gets it out of her room companion that Alice Gill did not sleep in her bed last night. Mrs Wells reasons that she could have run away or had an accident. She decides to have a look in the various places where the girl would have been working the previous evening. She finds her on the floor of the Old Library, realizes she's dead and rings the police office . . . By the way, has Superintendent Gardner been told yet?"

"No, sir," Botterell said. "He'll be on his way back from Windsor shortly with Their Majesties and I'll see him as soon as he gets here. I thought it unwise to break the news on the telephone."

The Commissioner agreed. "He'll have to be brought very much into the picture of course, but I've no doubt he has his hands full enough at the moment."

"In any case," the A.C. said, "the King's bodyguard has not had the necessary C.I.D. training. Deputy Commander Roe here is surely the man to take over."

"My own thoughts," the Commissioner nodded. "Now where were we . . . ? This housekeeper woman rings the police office. Botterell's man takes the call . . . Name, Chief Inspector?"

"Inspector Calkin, sir."

"Calkin rings the Palace doctor and they meet there in the library. Mrs Wells is told to report that Alice Gill has fallen off a stepladder and broken her neck. Chief Inspector Botterell has been fetched by now and he gets in touch with Scotland Yard—"

"Excuse me, Commissioner," the Master of the Household broke in. "Need it be a fatal accident? I think as far as Mrs Wells knows the girl fell off a stepladder and has concussion. Their Majesties would be upset if they were to hear of a death under their roof at a time when the whole country is getting ready to celebrate."

"I take your point," the Commissioner said. "But that of course will mean removing the body at a busy time of day—and by ambulance. What about the ambulance men?"

"I know the ones I could use," Botterell said. "They are both thoroughly reliable and there's no need for them to be told the full truth. We can't hide the fact they'll be removing a dead body, but I shall explain we don't want that known for the reason Sir Wilfred has just given."

"Can the injuries be covered?" the A.C. queried.

"Dr Flint is going to bandage them, sir, once the C.I.D. have finished what they have to do. Alice Gill can be carried out on a stretcher apparently still unconscious, with Dr Flint in attendance. Officially she will die in the ambulance and can be taken direct to the mortuary."

"Cutting out the King's Coroner," the Commissioner said with approval. "Yes indeed! I was anticipating a sticky time with old Abercrombie, but if the girl dies outside the Royal precincts . . . I'll settle for that. Now what about your men, Roe? What's the minimum strength you'll require in the way of assistance?"

Roe said, "I suppose at a pinch it can be managed by one photographer and one fingerprint man—much as it goes against the grain to skimp things when we're after the most wanted killer in my experience . . . And because of that very fact I wish I didn't have to say this, sir, but I feel I'm not the man to take over when we get the summons to the Palace."

All eyes held the speaker in surprise and concern. Deputy Commander William Roe, until his recent promotion chief of Scotland Yard's 382 detectives, was one of the few high-ranking officers at headquarters who had joined the Metropolitan Police as constable, though his authoritative bearing coupled with a bristling reddish moustache gave him a military look not shared by the ex-military Commissioner. Before taking up his present post he had won a reputation as a brilliant investigator of serious crime. Macabre statistics would probably have shown that none of his contemporaries came near to matching Roe of the Yard in providing work for the hangman. That he was the obvious choice to handle this most demanding of murder hunts had been assumed until this moment by the other four members of the worried group.

It took only a few seconds for the A.C. to see the light. "Your presence at the Palace?"

"Exactly, sir. In my present work I've become known to most of the Royal Family and many of the senior staff there. If any of them were to see me around I think there'd be questions asked. And I'm afraid the same applies to all top C.I.D. officers: why a bloke of such standing to investigate the death of an under-housemaid? It wouldn't be long before we'd have the Press on to it."

The Commissioner suppressed a shudder. "Somebody from the provinces then?"

"I'd prefer a man with some knowledge of the ground." Roe looked at Botterell. "You've had no experience of detective work, have you, Bob?"

"Sorry. Not even aid to C.I.D."

"Who do you have in mind, William?" The A.C. knew his man.

Roe said, "If the story we're putting out was true the investigation of that girl's death wouldn't rate anyone above the rank of detective sergeant."

"You're surely not suggesting we put a detective sergeant in charge of a case like this?" The Commissioner had the expression of one chary of being thought facetious in the circumstances.

"As a matter of fact, sir, I am." William Roe had surprised

them afresh to the extent of provoking total silence. "Officially, that is to say. I'm pretty sure the one I have in mind will do a first-rate job. He's a bright lad—going to end up with a department of his own unless I'm very much mistaken. If promotion here didn't involve that bloody British reverence for seniority he'd be at least an inspector by now."

"Bennett," the A.C. said without any question mark.

Roe nodded. "Harry Bennett."

"Ah, yes—Detective Sergeant Bennett." The Commissioner was with them now. "He's the one that did such fine work on the Kitteridge case."

"Right, sir. That and several others. And when I talk about putting Bennett in charge I don't mean that as we usually understand it. This is going to be a job like none we've ever tackled before, so it's no use falling back on the old routine. With your approval I shall be the one actually supervising the case with Bennett acting as my front man." He added tactfully, "With of course the valuable assistance of Superintendent Gardner and Chief Inspector Botterell."

One further moment of frowning thought and the Commissioner picked up a telephone. "We'd better see if he's in the building."

4

It has been said that top detectives have a tendency to resemble off-stage comedians, donning perhaps an armour of apparent insensitivity to protect their sanity against the ultimate in human baseness.

At 28 Harry Bennett had already had his share of that, but without as yet acquiring the features of a stand-up comic. He had, nevertheless, the kind of face that was ready to crinkle into amusement as an antidote to the nausea which, coupled with indigestion, is the occupational affliction of detectives.

Not that it was crinkling now. Instructed to go at once to the Commissioner's office as he was resigning himself to the boredom of finalizing a report on an indisputable manslaughter, Harry was still young enough to have knee-weakening memories of a summons to the headmaster's study at his Reading school.

He had been born and brought up in that Berkshire town. His father, a solicitor's clerk, prided himself on being responsible for the boy's affinity with the law; but in fact it had been the exploits of Sexton Blake, Nelson Lee and Sherlock Holmes which had set Harry on his determined course. Realizing early that the real-life private investigator sadly lacked the glamour of his fictional heroes, Harry made up his mind to join the police as soon as he left school. Nothing less of course than the Metropolitan Police, Scotland Yard being his goal. Accepted into 'C' Division, he spent the obligatory three years in uniform with strained patience, despite the sleazy streets of Soho offering more diversions than came the way of most constables on London beats.

A uniformed man's first application to be taken on C.I.D. strength was usually turned down as a matter of bloody-minded routine. Constable Bennett managed to dodge the system by virtue of his patent honesty and his nose for villainy. His section officer was the notorious Sergeant Goddard. Without sufficient proof of the corruption about him to turn informer, even if he could have brought himself to squeal on his fellow officers, Harry circumspectly put in for a change of section, his request being speedily granted.*

Emerging blameless from the shake-up that followed the subsequent exposure and jailing of his former sergeant, Harry, to his pleased surprise, found himself on plain clothes patrol within a month of his application receiving the Chief Constable's nod. He passed his preliminary examinations one year later, and the far more difficult one for promotion to detective-sergeant by the time he was twenty-five. Achieving shortly afterwards his long-held ambition to become a Scotland Yard man, he had the good fortune to serve here under the great William Roe.

*It is conceivable that H.B. was the writer of the anonymous letters that led to Goddard's downfall but this seems doubtful. Covert recrimination was not H.B.'s style.

The recent Kitteridge case had brought him a Commissioner's commendation. Bernard Kitteridge shot dead the woman he was living with in Camden Town and disappeared with her 13-year-old daughter. By skilful deduction Harry Bennett traced him to an address in Croydon, where Kitteridge barricaded himself on the top floor, holding the child hostage and threatening to shoot any policeman who approached within range. In five tense and exhausting hours Harry 'talked' him—by means of a megaphone —into releasing the girl and later giving himself up: a considerable feat at a time when a murderer's surrender was tantamount to suicide.

Half an hour with the distinguished company in the Commissioner's office on this first morning of May left Harry Bennett even weaker at the knees and in a state of exhilaration he knew to be shameful. Astonishment at being picked for a job of such importance had been swiftly followed by understanding of why the choice had to fall on a detective of his humble rank. It was an unprecedented opportunity, against which must be set the certainty that failure would blight the rest of his career. To bungle the hunt for a murderer at large under the King's own roof would damn him for ever in the eyes of these powerful men so agonizingly forced to rely on him.

Yet never had one of his kind been faced with such handicaps as he went about his work. Nearly all the precepts of his training would need to be broken for the investigation of a murder that was officially nothing of the sort: essential questioning to be so guarded as never to reveal the truth; search for clues to be carried out as nearly as possible in secrecy; no support from the Press, no public appeal to bring hoped-for response; expert assistance cut to the minimum . . .

"Who am I allowed to take with me, sir?" Harry was relieved to find his voice retaining a reasonable steadiness.

Roe said, "Duncan for pictures, Spencer for tabs. You'll also have one assistant from the women's branch."

"Miss Knight?"

The A.C. and Roe exchanged glances as a prediction was borne out. They had discussed this while awaiting Bennett's arrival. Women police had yet to be trained for C.I.D. work, but a few of them were borrowed on occasion to perform specialized duties.

W.P.C. Knight had distinguished herself under the most dis-
agreeable and dangerous conditions on a case handled by
William Roe with Harry Bennett assisting. She was an attractive
girl and Harry was a single man, but Roe was satisfied that
nothing outside this vastly important case would impair the
efficiency of their renewed partnership.

He nodded. "Miss Knight. She will be joining the Palace staff
in the dead girl's place. Sir Wilfred Jennings will see to it there
are no difficulties about that."

A confirmatory nod from the Master of the Household. Roe
looked impatiently at his watch and addressed the Commissioner. "I think, sir, we ought to get moving. With your
permission I'd like to run through it all again with Sergeant
Bennett in my office while Chief Inspector Botterell is making his
way back to the Palace."

It remained only for the pair to be wished all the luck they were
undoubtedly going to need. The meeting broke up at 9.20 a.m.

The first recorded call to the Yard from Chief Inspector
Botterell came twenty minutes later and was taken by Detective
Constable Stevens as Harry was re-entering his office.

"Accidental death at Buckingham Palace. Maid fell off a
ladder, broke her neck. No suspicious circumstances but they
want it kept quiet."

"I'm not surprised. Nasty thing to happen at a time like this.
All right, tell 'em I'll be along." It irked Harry to have to deceive
Tom Stevens, his trusted sidekick.

"Want me to come with you, Sarge?"

"No need, Tom. Royal residence—they'll only want a routine
checkup."

It was 9.52 a.m. The strangest, least heard of, yet most vital
murder hunt of the century was in progress.

5

In his off-duty hours Chief Inspector Robert Botterell liked to
sink a pint or two at the Bag O'Nails in Buckingham Palace Road.
A good friend among his fellow regulars there was Jim Rennie,

an ambulance driver attached to Westminster Hospital, a quiet solid, pipe-smoking man of Botterell's own age. Sometimes they were joined by Rennie's partner on the ambulance, another quiet middle-aged man also called Jim whose surname Botterell either hadn't heard or couldn't remember. The three had also met now and then in the course of their respective duties, the two Jims having visited Buckingham Palace to remove the victim of an accident in the kitchens or a fainting guardsman injured by falling on his bayonet. As Botterell had told the Commissioner, he was confident that reliance could be placed on their discretion and he prayed they might be available this morning to undertake this trickiest of operations; if not, he was prepared to have them dragged out of bed whatever time they might have signed off last night.

His prayer was answered. Jim Rennie was on duty and at hand to speak to him on the telephone. Botterell's request for a standby was granted without undue questioning, the gravity of his tone perhaps making the impression denied to his tongue.

Everything indeed had so far gone as smoothly as could have been hoped. Inspector Calkin, returning to the Old Library after breaking the news to the shocked Palace Steward, had been troubled by no would-be entrant up to the time when Mrs Wells was instructed to remake her discovery of three hours ago. The assistant housekeeper had meanwhile had Alice Gill's room companion up in front of her. "Clara Watson. Stupid lump of a girl. Tried at first to lie about it, then burst into tears and admitted she hadn't seen Gill since tea last evening." Botterell could not help feeling some sympathy for Clara Watson, who at a guess had been subjected to a third degree questioning that would not have been countenanced at any British police station.

Mrs Wells went after that to report the girl's absence to Mrs Percival, the Palace housekeeper, who showed scant interest in the information. A lady of majestic bearing with an imposing grey-fringed hairdo, Mrs Percival modelled herself on Queen Mary so closely as almost to risk a charge of impersonation. With the Silver Jubilee less than a week away and many distinguished guests due to be graciously received, Mrs Percival gave her assistant to understand that she ought not to have been bothered by the trifling matter of a runaway housemaid. "Have the gel replaced. If she comes back we don't want her." Mrs Wells left the presence chastened, though her humiliation was mitigated by the inward glow of secret knowledge. If the haughty old bitch only knew what she did . . . .

Upon Botterell's return to the Palace Mrs Wells was sent to retrace her steps of the early morning. Calkin admitted her to the Old Library in response to a pre-arranged knock. Mrs Wells made a brief pretence of examining the dead girl before picking up the telephone. So far but for Calkin's presence it might have been the re-run of a motion picture, the action changing only when it was Chief Inspector Botterell who this time took her call to the police office. Dr Flint, also awaiting his summons, then joined the other three in the library and re-examined the body, reporting the *rigor* now complete.

Detective Sergeant Bennett and his two assistants met Botterell in the latter's office some ten minutes later. The task of conducting them unobtrusively with their equipment to the scene of murder was facilitated by the kind of week it was. Much of the furniture at Buckingham Palace was seedy in the extreme and over the past month a number of the most shameful pieces had been scrapped and replaced in honour of Their Majesties' twenty-five years' reign; thus workmen bearing old furniture or replacements were a familiar sight in the one and a half miles of corridors. Bennett's men, Duncan and Spencer, were fitted with green baize aprons and given a hastily emptied chest of drawers to carry. In this and in their jackets they concealed cameras, fingerprinting materials and one of Scotland Yard's eight famous 'murder bags' kept ready packed with all conceivable aids to detection.

Getting Harry Bennett himself to the library presented more of a problem. Once Alice Gill's death became known it would be understandable for a detective sergeant to be sent from Scotland Yard to satisfy the authorities that there had been no foul play; but for him to be seen around while the girl was supposed to be unconscious but still alive might cause the perceptive to indulge in dangerous speculation. It was decided that Harry should be labelled a temporary addition to Superintendent Gardner's staff for security purposes during this auspicious week; as a trained C.I.D. man fortuitously on the spot at the time of the accident, it would not be unreasonable for him to undertake the necessary investigation.

Botterell took him across the quadrangle to the entrance used by Cabinet Ministers for their audiences with the King. The Palace Steward, Brian Goodship, was awaiting them in his private quarters, situated near the top of the Ministers' Staircase. Mr Goodship was an irascible, constantly worried man of 50, his tendency to frowning exacerbated by the wrinkled relics of many years' Government service in India. Persons of authority with Mr Goodship's temperament are inclined to fly off the handle in near panic at times of crisis; Mr Goodship was an exception in that his temper, though permanently simmering, was never permitted to boil over. Worry was so much a part of his life that he would have regarded any recession of it as a token of inefficiency and thus given himelf fresh cause to worry. He was not a popular man but the Palace staff considered him a fair one and seldom questioned the opinion of those above him that it would be hard to find a more competent administrator and organizer.

Harry Bennett, who had the detective's consciousness that a wasted minute could be an irredeemable loss, was pleased to find Mr Goodship dispensing with unnecessary comment on the disaster. "You'll naturally have to talk to people. You could of course use one of my offices for your interviews but I don't advise it. Make your business look too important. Mrs Wells being in on it, I'd say the best place would be her private sitting-room."

Harry warmed to the man for taking his intended words out of his mouth. "I agree, sir. How far is that from where we are now?"

"Quite a way. Will that matter? Once you've finished in the Old Library—"

"I have in mind," Harry said, "the necessary break in our work there. We three detectives mustn't be in evidence when the girl is taken away."

"Ah, by the ambulance men—I get you. Suggest you slip in here while that goes on—shift the old chest of drawers again in case some nosey person wonders who you all are." Harry realized that the capable mind of Brian Goodship had been behind that particular subterfuge.

Their work in the Old Library was comparatively brief up to

the time of the break. Dr Flint gave it as his opinion that there had been no attempt at sexual assault, and from the condition of Alice Gill's outer garments Harry was in agreement. She carried in her single uniform pocket only a crumpled hankie. There was no evidence that she had put up a fight. Two splashes of blood on the half-drawn curtains suggested the attacker had awaited the girl from behind them and taken her by surprise, possibly striking at least the first blow there and later dragging the fallen body to where it now lay.

So why not make a better job of setting the scene for a fall from the ladder? Perhaps came the belated realization that multiple blows would tell a different story; or it could have been anxiety to leave the scene of the crime as rapidly as possible while the corridor was still clear.

But all of this was little more than theory. Clothes, curtains and strip of carpet as well as the body itself would shortly be submitted to the forensic experts for what valuable information they might provide.

Harry straightened up from the stiffened body. "All right, Doctor, she's yours. Do your best not to disturb the wounds more than you can help."

The detectives withdrew to Brian Goodship's rooms. Dr Flint applied his bandages while Botterell went to brief and bring up the two ambulance men. The Chief Inspector's confidence in them was justified by their immediate understanding and compliance with the deception—as far as they were themselves aware of it.

Accompanied by the doctor, they were barely half a dozen paces out of the library when there took place one of the chance encounters feared by those in possession of the full truth. A door opened ahead of them and Lady Wittlesham's maid came out of her employer's apartment. Having recently treated Miss Ethel Currie for a poisoned thumb Dr Flint knew her to be compulsively talkative and so almost certainly a gossip.

The lady's maid came to a wide-eyed halt. "Good gracious, what's happened?"

"Poor girl's had a fall," Flint said. "One of the housemaids."

The stretcher bearers had sensibly not checked but the tiresome woman kept pace with them.

"Who is it? Oh—it's Alice, isn't it. Is she bad?"

"Shan't know till we get her to hospital. She's had a nasty bang on the head. Now please don't hold us up, Miss Currie." It was the only way to shake her off.

They reached the ground floor and went out through the Ambassadors' Entrance without being conscious of any more prying eyes. The ambulance was already parked here, and at 11.17 a.m. on this bright May morning 20-year-old Alice Gill went for her last ride through the gaily bedecked streets to the grisly place where impersonal specialists waited to take her literally to pieces.

Within ten minutes the Palace Steward received a telephone call from the Press Officer to the Royal Household.

"I have the Press Association on the line. Somebody just saw an ambulance leaving the Palace. What's the story?"

"Hardly what they'd call a story," Brian Goodship said evenly. "Housemaid had a tumble, gave herself a crack on the head."

"Where was this? In the Royal quarters? Any of the Family see it happen?"

"Good heavens, no. I doubt if this girl has ever risen to those heights. She's young and fairly new here. There's not a damned thing in it for any of your contacts."

"O.K.—but you might let me know in future, Mr Goodship, if anything like this happens. I feel such a bloody fool if I don't know what to tell 'em."

"Sure, sure—but I'd have thought we were both too damned busy this week to waste our time over piddling affairs like this." Mr Goodship had to restrain himself from slamming down the receiver. This was clearly going to be a double hell of a day in what was already a hellish week.

The same sentiments were being expressed in the Old Library where the meticulous and onerous search for clues was continuing. "Prints galore," Spencer reported, "but I don't expect we'll find any of 'em in Records, not from a place like this."

"Except for the Prince of Wales," Harry reminded him. "Didn't he have his taken when he paid that visit of his to the Yard?"

"Right enough, Sarge. But something tells me it wasn't the Pagger Wagger that bumped off our poor little housemaid."

All available prints had nevertheless to be taken and checked on the off-chance that one of them might be identified in the bureau's files, or in case any of them later matched up with those of a suspect.

It was midday before the three detectives completed this first stage of their work. Still missing was potentially one of the most important clues, the murder weapon. It could of course be still in the room, hidden in a space between books and wall. To undertake the task of lifting out some eight thousand volumes Charles Calkin was left alone with his sardonic thoughts. By far the biggest job any of them was likely ever to be involved in, yet with a chief inspector subservient to a sergeant, and an inspector doing the chore of a mere constable, it had to be tackled arse upward . . .

6

At about the time when the slight shapely figure of Alice Gill became the centre of forensic attention, W.P.C. Veronica Knight left her West Hampstead flat to pick up her second-hand Austin Seven and drive the fifteen-odd miles to Watford, where the dead girl's mother lived.

For Veronica it had been no less startling a morning than for the dozen or so others entrusted with the true facts of what had occurred at Buckingham Palace around eight o'clock the previous evening. She had herself been on late turn at that time and should have signed off at 10 p.m. With barely five minutes to go, a young woman had an epileptic fit while leaving a Kilburn cinema. By the time Veronica had seen her removed to hospital, found out her name and address, arranged with neighbours to look after her two small children, returned to the station, written the necessary report and had a late snack in the canteen it was well past midnight.

Dropping exhausted into bed after her ten hours' tour of duty, she had pressed the stopper firmly down on her alarm clock, only to be awakened a few minutes after 9 a.m. by a constable of her

'S' Division hammering on her flat door at the same time as he kept a finger pressed on the bell push. Veronica dragged herself to the door and opened it, not caring about her appearance.

"Heavens, Wally—is it war, revolution or merely an earthquake?"

"You might prefer all three, love. It's the big sod himself, Deputy Commander William Roe. You're to get to the Yard pronto."

"Oh no, not again! Did he say why?"

"Tell the likes of us? Don't be a berk. Get your clothes on quick, we've got the car outside. And he said plain clothes, meaning I reckon they want you sexy again."

"If it's anything like last time I'd sooner stay in that ghastly uniform," Veronica said as she hastened back into her bedroom.

As late as 1935 London's policewomen were still issued with a uniform that might have been designed to deter any girl who cared about her looks from joining the force. Veronica Knight was one of the exceptions: an attractive girl whose sense of humour and attachment to her work enabled her to laugh off the imposition of appearing in public like the stern matron of a Dickensian workhouse, her rich fair hair hidden under a hat like a large upturned porridge plate.

She was country bred. Her father, a market gardener in a village near Canterbury, named his three daughters after flowers. Not for him however the conventional Rose or Iris: his girls were Petunia, Godetia and Veronica. In adolescence all three had had stage ambitions. At 16 Petunia achieved hers, getting into the chorus of a Chatham pantomime. Three years later, still a chorus girl, she had to beg the money for a telegram home to announce her abandonment in Sunderland by the ubiquitous decamping manager.

All dreams of a stage career thereupon ceased in the Knight family. Petunia became a barmaid in Canterbury and married the publican's son. Godetia went to Canada as a children's nurse. Veronica joined the Metropolitan Police.

She was now 23, handsome rather than pretty, with a figure which caused her some half-hearted attempts at dieting, though no male eyes saw the need for it. ("You stay nice and cuddly," said her station sergeant.) In conjunction with an amiable face, the features without perceptible flaw, it gave her an appeal to men (when she was out of uniform) that had evidently been noticed on high and led to her being picked last autumn for temporary transfer to Scotland Yard, where she was offered "special duties of a delicate nature". It was airily explained that she had the right to refuse to oblige, but Veronica was left in no doubt as to the resulting scornful disappointment in her were she to do so.

A known ponce was believed to be a leading figure behind the importing of cocaine into the country, some of which was being supplied to West End streetwalkers. For three weeks and a day Veronica became one of them, hair cheaply permed, make-up crudely applied, handbag carried at the trail. Nobody penetrated her disguise. Arrested once for soliciting by a constable unaware of her identity, she was fined £2 at Bow Street. It was not long before her quarry made himself known to her, but she had to suffer the ordeal for two more weeks before the Yard was satisfied that she had obtained enough evidence to ensure a conviction. The man went down for five years. Veronica received commendations from both Judge and Commissioner. The extent to which she had played her part in her rented Soho room was something that no living soul would ever drag out of her.

Relief was her first emotion this morning after she had heard what Deputy Commander William Roe had to tell her. The realization that her next 'special duties' could bear no relation to her previous experience was swiftly followed by indignation at the setting of the crime and determination to do all in her power to help bring down its perpetrator. She was given no opportunity this time to back out, Roe rightly taking it for granted that she had only to be told what was demanded of her.

"You'll report this afternoon to Mrs Wells, the assistant house-keeper. You won't need references, she's expecting you, but you must have a cover story prepared for other members of the staff who'll want to know where you come from and where you've worked before. Your job is to collect every possible piece of information about Alice Gill and why somebody might want to kill her. But make very sure you don't seem unduly curious. Detective Sergeant Bennett will of course be a stranger to you until he gets a chance to confer with you alone. Leave it to him to arrange your meetings."

"Do I use a false name, sir?"

"No real need for that, it can sometimes be a handicap. I suggest we shorten yours a bit—Vera sounds more appropriate than Veronica. But you'd better have another name for what you'll be doing before you go to the Palace."

Veronica was surprised. "I thought you said this afternoon—"

"I did. But you're going to be busy this morning too. I don't know whether they have a welfare officer attached to the Buck House staff, but that's what I'm appointing you now. Normally I'd be putting somebody else on to this, but with security so tight we have to do some doubling. I want you to visit Alice Gill's home in Watford, see what you can pick up there. I understand she leaves a widowed mother. The local police will have broken the news by the time you get there, so you'll simply be a follow-up." Roe looked critically at the printed silk dress Veronica had bought last month at Selfridge's to add to the gaiety of Jubilee Week. "I hope you have something to wear a little more suited to the occasion."

Veronica reassured him as to that, later regretting the impulsiveness that deprived her of a new outfit bought from police funds.

"You have a car of your own I believe. Use that and put in for expenses. Best you aren't seen arriving in a police car. Go back home now, change your clothes, pack what you'll need for your stay at the Palace—I hope to God it won't be too long—and wait then for our call. You'll be warned once the girl has been officially pronounced dead. Allow say a good ninety minutes after that before you visit the mother."

The telephone rang in Veronica's flat at 11.40 a.m. as she sat waiting in navy blue coat and skirt with white blouse and a severe grey hat bought with a suppressed shudder on her way back from Scotland Yard. The message was precise and as predicted: "Subject died in ambulance. Local police informed. Proceed as instructed."

She drove with deliberate lack of hurry through the flag-festooned streets and the pleasant patches of countryside that still at this date lay between the metropolis and the market town of Watford. Her stop at the police station here was fortuitously

timed, coinciding with the return of a middle-aged policewoman from breaking the news of the fatal 'accident' to Mrs
Hanson, as the former Mrs Gill was now.

"Not a woman I'd ordinarily take to, but one has to feel sorry
for her. It's only six weeks since she lost her second husband.
Actually, between you and me, I doubt if she's quite so upset this
time for all the floods of tears. She hadn't seen or heard from
Alice for nearly two years. Her married daughter is with her
now, a Mrs Willis. Lives only a few streets away, so I went and
fetched her."

Veronica found the address without difficulty from the other
policewoman's directions. It was one of a row of mean little
Victorian houses within unfortunate earshot of Watford's football ground. Twisted railings in front of the tiny patch of untended garden bore evidence of Saturday crowd pressure. A
faded Union Jack was draped along them and a cardboard cut-
out in the front window wished long life to the King and Queen
who stared stiffly at each other from photographic ovals set
against a red, white and blue background.

Mrs Hanson was a short stout woman with a large quivering
face and black hair streaked with grey, worn in the shape of a
cottage loaf. She sat sobbing in her kitchen over the inevitable
cup of tea, kept replenished by her elder daughter, a sensible
little woman in her late twenties.

"Why does it all have to happen to me? Two husbands and
now my little girl, it isn't fair. What have I done to deserve
it?—tell me that. I've always tried to live good and decent . . . "

Hilda Willis checked the effusion with a comforting arm.
"Now, now, Mum, I'm sure this lady understands how you feel,
but we want to know just what happened to poor dear Alice,
don't we now." And to Veronica, "The policewoman said she fell
off a ladder, that's all we've been told. What was my young sister
doing up a ladder for heaven's sake?—in a place like Buckingham Palace."

"It was in one of the libraries," Veronica said. "They have
these ladders to get at books that are out of reach. I gather Alice
was dusting along one of the high shelves and she must have lost
her balance. She hit herself on the head and was unconscious
when they found her. She never came round, so she couldn't

have suffered. The doctor travelled with her in the ambulance to
do all he could, but I'm afraid she passed away before they could
reach the hospital." God forgive me, Veronica said silently, for
feeding these monstrous lies to a bereaved mother.

A minute later the bereaved mother made her feel better about
it.

"Accident at work—that'll mean compensation, won't it?
About time I had something from that job of hers. Never a penny
sent home, not for nearly two years now."

"Didn't you speak to her about that?" Veronica welcomed the
opening to learn more of the split between them.

"She never give me the chance, didn't even come to my Reg's
funeral. It was news to me she'd gone to work for the King, Hilda
here had to tell me that. She wasn't a good daughter, Miss,
though I didn't ought to be saying that now. My poor little girl
laying there dead . . . "

It was only after Hilda Willis had prevailed on her mother to go
to her bed that Veronica gained any of the information she
sought. Hilda and a brother now in Australia were, like Alice,
the children of Percy Gill who had been badly wounded at
Passchendaele and crippled for the rest of his short sad life.

"There was a lot he couldn't do for himself and Mum isn't what
you'd call the most patient of women. He had a job of sorts at the
British Legion club, polishing glasses and setting out the
snooker balls, but it didn't bring in much and then he had to give
that up. They was cat and dog half the time, I couldn't bear it, I
left home soon as I could and went into service. I'm eight years
older than Alice. She adored her dad, always took his part when
they were at it and got her ears boxed more than once, I can tell
you. She took it bad when he died. That'd be about six or seven
years ago when she was still at school. Then about a year later
Mum married Reg Hanson. He'd been left a widower, worked all
his life at Benson's, the grocers in the High Street. I thought
myself he wasn't a bad old stick, he seemed nice and gentle. My
husband liked him too, but Alice couldn't abide him."

"Because he'd taken her father's place?"

Mrs Willis paused briefly. "There could have been more than
that to it—I don't know. I never did know for sure. She said he
used to interfere with her, let his hand wander up where it

didn't ought."

"Did you believe that?"

"Couldn't ever make our minds up, Fred and me. He didn't seem the type. Used to say his prayers at night and went to chapel regular on Sundays, but then you can't ever tell with them sort, can you? Alice swore blind to it, only she doesn't always speak the truth . . . Didn't, I mean." A sob. "I'm sorry, she was my little sister."

"If talking about her distresses you—"

Veronica realized belatedly that she had been injudicious in her consideration; but to her relief Hilda shook her head.

"It's all right, we weren't all that close, too many years between us. And I'd like you to know why Mum sounded—well, a bit heartless. She did have a lot to put up with from Alice."

"Did Alice tell her what her stepfather had been up to?"

"In the end, yes. But that was after Alice left home. She went into service like me when she was only fifteen."

"Here in Watford?"

"No, in London. She was with a Mrs Garrett in Holland Park. Used to come home now and then on her days off. Came mostly to see Fred and me, but living so near I said it wouldn't be right for her not to go and look Mum up. Pity I did as it turned out. I'd made her promise she wouldn't say a word to Mum about Reg and his naughty little ways. Mum thought the world of her Reg and I was glad to see her happy at last. Then some silly little row blew up when Alice was there on one of her visits—Reg ticked her off for the way she spoke to her mother and that did it. Alice lost her temper and broke her promise. Said Reg wasn't nothing but a dirty old man and came out with all the stuff about his wandering hands when she was still a little schoolgirl. He denied it of course and Mum believed him, knowing Alice was a bit of a one for telling stories. She chucked her out of the house and told her never to come back unless she admitted she was a liar and apologized to Reg. Alice took her at her word. She still came to see Fred and me, though not so often this last year or two, but she never showed her face in this house again, not even after I told her Reg had died."

"That was after she'd gone to work at Buckingham Palace."

"Yes. She was four years with Mrs Garrett, then she met this chap who's a footman there and he told her they was taking on extra maids for Jubilee Year, so she went for an interview and got accepted. She's not been getting as much as Mrs Garrett paid her, but that didn't seem to worry her. Said she liked the honour of working for the King and Queen, but this footman bloke could have been the chief reason, I don't know."

"Which of our footmen was it?" A studied tone betraying only mild interest. "I'm sure he'll be very upset."

"Couldn't tell you, I'm afraid," Hilda said frustratingly. "I suppose she might have mentioned his name, but if she did I never took it in."

"Never mind, I daresay I can find out when I get back there." Veronica dismissed it as of small consequence and their talk became practical. She explained that funeral arrangements would have to await the inevitable inquest. They must not worry about the cost: Royalty looked after its loyal servants. (Did it? No matter: Royalty was committed now. As one of the few who had been let in on the dread secret she had the power to see that her promise was made good.)

She left Watford hating her job almost as much as she had hated it once before. It had turned her into a liar and a fraud, an exploiter of these trusting people at their time of distress. Her only solace was consciousness that her behaviour was more than justified by the mighty issue dependent on it, that there might yet be real value in the scraps of information she had drawn from Hilda Willis. Guilt must be supplanted by pride that she, Veronica Knight, had been picked to play an essential part in this momentous real-life drama.

Whore yesterday, welfare officer today, housemaid tomorrow: it seemed that she had been somewhat premature in abandoning that long-ago ambition to become an actress.

7

The experienced detective is almost immune to surprise, but Harry Bennett could be said to have been at least taken aback by his first sight of a housemaids' bedroom in the nation's No. 1

residence. The room contained two chipped iron bedsteads, a double washstand, a shared chest of drawers; cheap coverings on the thinnest of mattresses; a brass bar and a row of hooks behind faded curtains to serve as a shared wardrobe; a pair of cane chairs; a single drab window curtain terminating six inches short of the sill. Under each bed beside the article that was still a euphemism for chamber pot there was an article of luggage: Clara Watson's of basketware, Alice Gill's a tin trunk.

Lighting was restricted to a 40-watt bulb hanging unshaded from the ceiling and operated by a switch outside in the corridor which also served the next bedroom. Some architect of the distant past with humanitarian ideas had equipped the room with chimney and fireplace. Not surprisingly, the grate was bare—and Harry wondered when, if ever, a housemaid last laid and lit a fire for herself in Buckingham Palace.

He had been accompanied to the room by Clara Watson, whom he had first met in Mrs Wells's sitting-room ten minutes earlier. The assistant housekeeper had demurred at his request for Clara to conduct him there on her own—a house rule prohibited a mixing of the sexes in any bedroom. Harry had to be firm with her; it was plain from a glance at Clara Watson that he'd get little out of this one in the presence of so formidable a superior. In calling her a stupid lump Mrs Wells had been unkind but perhaps had not exaggerated unduly. Clara was a heavily built girl with a round, simple face and thick petulant lips. Her sullen expression had not perceptibly changed when in Harry's presence Mrs Wells had broken the news of Alice's death.

"It's my job to go through her belongings before handing them over to her family," he had told the girl. "You see, we have to satisfy the coroner at the inquest that her death was purely accidental." Harry was all too conscious of the *non sequitur*, but Clara appeared to accept it as coming from Authority and thus not to be queried. "I want you to come with me," he continued, "just to make sure I touch nothing of yours, only what belonged to Alice." Clara glanced uncertainly at Mrs Wells and received a frigid nod. "Will you please show me the way, Clara?"

It had been a silent walk through the forbidding corridors of the lower servants' quarters. "I'm afraid this must be very distressing for you," Harry said as the girl pointed out the long and the short drawer containing Alice's property.

A shrug. "Not specially."

"Oh. I thought girls who shared a room usually became fairly close friends."

"I didn't ask to share with that one." A lengthy pause, with Harry careful to give his outward attention to the uninformative contents of the two drawers. "I didn't like her."

"But you tried to help her all the same, didn't you? Telling Mrs Wells she slept here last night. I think that was pretty decent of you, doing it for a girl you didn't like." He turned to the curtained hanging space.

"I didn't know then she wasn't coming back, did I?"

A purse in a pocket of an outdoor coat. He let Clara see him open it. "You were afraid of Alice? Is that why you lied for her?"

"Naow! 'Course I wasn't afraid, not of her. Only of what she might do."

A shilling, two sixpences, a threepenny bit, two pennies and a key. Harry took the key out. "Would this be the key to that trunk of hers?"

"I s'pose so. That's where she kept her other things."

"You were afraid of what she might do . . . What might she have done if you hadn't tried to protect her?"

"I dunno. Ripped me dress, I wouldn't be surprised. Or done what she done once before—if she dared."

"What was that?" He was purposely fumbling the fitting of the key into the lock of the trunk.

"Emptied me pot into me bed and tried to make out I'd done a wet."

"Nasty! What did you do about that, Clara?"

"I clipped her one," and with undisguised satisfaction, "made her nose bleed."

"I don't blame you." A hefty girl with perhaps in her own simple outlook a motive for dealing out more than a bloodied nose . . . He had been too ready thus far to assume it was a man they were looking for. "What was the trouble about that time?"

"My business." She gave him a searching glance. "You're a nosey one, aren't you!"

Danger . . . Time to temper the probing. He chuckled. "So

I've been told before. I'm sorry. But when people have had a shock it sometimes helps to get them talking. And it must have been a shock for you, hearing your room mate was dead, even if you didn't like her." He turned the key, swung back the lid of the trunk. "You didn't knock her off that ladder in the Old Library, I suppose?"

"Might have done if I'd bin there."

No, he was getting too fanciful: he'd wager a month's pay against a double bluff like that from this one.

More clothes in the trunk, unmistakably, even to his male eye, of better quality that those left in the open. "I imagine these were what she wore on her days off?"

"Never took that much notice."

"Wanting to look her best for some young man . . . Did she have a regular one?"

"She was a tart!"

"Played the field, did she?" A few trifling possessions hardly worth a second glance, a shiny black imitation leather handbag. "Know any of her chaps, do you? They ought to be told what happened."

In the bag were a Post Office savings book, an open envelope addressed 'To whom it may concern'—a reference, he guessed.

Clara was silent. He looked up at her. "What did you think when she didn't come back last night? Spending it with a man— is that what you thought?"

"I wondered. She got a letter in the morning."

Interesting . . . "There's no letter here."

"No, she burnt it. I come in and saw her, burning it down in that grate there. We're not allowed fires in the room. I told her there'd be a row if Miss Carter saw that."

"Miss Carter?"

"Ellen Carter, our head housemaid. Alice said, 'All right, clear it up then.' Just like her bleeding sauce, giving *me* orders. But I knew we'd both catch it—'cause I couldn't split on her, could I?—so I got down on me knees and cleared it up for the lazy cat."

"Well, we know now she wasn't planning to go out last night. It was probably to arrange some future meeting."

Or a rendezvous in the library when she went there to draw the curtains? Mustn't put an idea like that into Clara's head.

Harry decided it was time to leave future probing to the room's next occupant. Poor Veronica! She didn't have much joy when it came to sleeping out.

He closed the trunk and straightened up. "You'd better be getting back to your work, Clara. Thanks for your help. I think I have all the facts I need for the Coroner."

She turned at the door she had just opened, half closing it again. "Dirty little bitch. God paid her out."

Left alone, Harry reopened the trunk and handbag. Between the pages of the savings book were seven pound notes and two ten-shilling notes. Her account showed a credit of £43. 4s. 4d. The sum of £40 had been deposited on 27 March, five weeks ago. Miss Alice Gill had undoubtedly found a means of supplementing her housemaid's wages of £45 per annum.

The envelope, as he had anticipated, contained a reference, written in an educated hand on notepaper with embossed address:

62 Monksfield Terrace
London W14

Alice Gill has been a housemaid in my employ for nearly four years. She is clean, honest, hard-working and of good moral character. I shall be sorry to lose her.

Audrey Garrett (Mrs Henry S. Garrett)

Harry moved to the fireplace and knelt. Clara Watson had unfortunately made a good job of clearing up the burnt letter. He gripped and gently raised the heavy iron cradle on which no coals were ever laid. Three—no, four—tiny scraps of black charred paper had found their way through the bars. Harry replaced the cradle taking extreme care not to disturb them.

Finding his way down to the police office while trying to memorize the way back was not easy; Harry wished he could leave chalk marks on the walls of the grim corridors.

Having handed Alice Gill's documents to Chief Inspector Botterell for immediate delivery to Roe at Scotland Yard, Harry applied himself to the murder bag brought down from the Old Library by Inspector Calkin, whose search behind its books had proved wholly abortive. He took from the bag two glass pans, a printing frame and an atomizer containing a mixture of shellac and alcohol such as was used as a fixative by artists on charcoal drawings. "This may take me some little time, it has to be done with a bloody hell of a lot of patience," he explained. "But if I manage to get something for the lab boys to work on, it'll need a steady hand to take it to them."

The Sergeant's voice of authority brought a sigh from the Inspector as he caught the Chief Inspector's eye.

Back in the housemaids' bedroom—after twice losing his way there despite the determined memorizing—Harry checked that the window was firmly closed, then took a blanket from Alice's bed to shut off the draught beneath the door. He propped a chair under the door handle as a precaution against its sudden opening. Kneeling again in front of the grate he again lifted the iron cradle, holding his breath as he very slowly turned and laid it down with the care of a mother for a delicate infant. To his relief the four vital scraps of burnt paper remained where they had been lying when first spotted.

Taking one of the glass pans in his left hand, Harry placed it as close as he dared to the flimsy black fragments. With a stiff sheet of paper he set about gently fanning them until he had moved all four intact on to the glass pan. He moistened them with the atomizer, then cautiously pressed them between glass with his second pan, finally clamping the pans into the printing frame.

Twenty-five precious minutes had passed by the time he regained his feet. He hoped to God the result was going to be worth it.

8

Deputy Commander William Roe looked up from the notes he had been making as W.P.C. Knight concluded her report.

"Pity you couldn't get that footman's name. Still, I daresay you'll find it out easily enough from the other servants—if not earlier."

"Earlier, sir?"

"Something else has come up for you to cover before they take you on at the Palace. Had any lunch yet?"

"No, sir. I came straight here from Watford."

"Have to do some slimming today, I'm afraid. This is urgent." Roe passed her a sheet of notepaper. "Alice Gill's reference. Sergeant Bennett found it among her belongings." And as Veronica read it, "Quite a treasure according to that lady."

Veronica nodded. "She seems to have appreciated poor Alice more than her mother did."

"If that's genuine—which is what you're to find out. Show it to Mrs Garrett, talk to any of her other servants who knew Alice. As far as they are concerned she's been reported missing and you can be yourself again—the policewoman appointed to make inquiries. You'll be interested to know, incidentally, that our Alice wasn't short of money. Forty-odd pounds in the post office and eight more in cash."

Veronica's eyebrows went up. "On the game? A royal servant?"

Roe shrugged. "Your guess is as good as mine—or perhaps better." And when she winced, "I'm sorry, Miss Knight, that was uncalled for. Now off you go to Monksfield Terrace and call back here on your way to your new job."

Monksfield Terrace was a highly rated street of three-storied Victorian houses, each with first-floor balcony and pillared porch; behind the spear-headed railings a steep flight of area steps led down to the inevitably dark basement. Number 62, at the Kensington end, backed on to Holland Park and had the well-kept appearance of—Veronica's guess—the home of a prosperous stockbroker and family. (She was not far out: Mr Henry S. Garrett was in fact a Lloyds underwriter).

Mrs Audrey Garrett was plump and fair, perhaps 45 though still retaining much of the sultry prettiness of one accustomed to being spoilt. She assumed an air of surprise that anyone in her position might be expected to supply the police with useful information about a missing domestic.

"I really can't see what I can possibly tell you, I'd almost forgotten the girl, she left here—oh, it's months ago. An ungrateful little hussy, I took her on quite untrained and she had no hesitation about leaving me in the lurch when it suited her. In a way I suppose I have only myself to blame—I wouldn't have engaged the child if I'd guessed she was going to turn out so pretty. I prefer a maid without followers like the plain little creature I've managed to replace her with."

You are pathetic, Veronica thought: a silly woman trying to impress by aping your betters of an age well past. Aloud she said, "Do you happen to know who any of those followers were?"

A tinkling laugh of insincere amusement. "Good heavens no, why on earth should I? All I know is that Alice lost her head over some footman she met at the Servants' Ball and he was on the Buckingham Palace staff and so that was where she promptly had to go. I daresay one of my other servants might be able to tell you more."

"Thank you. I'd like to speak to them in a minute."

"Is anything missing from the Palace apart from the girl herself?" Mrs Garrett asked curiously. "She's not under suspicion?"

Veronica shook her head. "Nothing like that, we just want to know what's happened to her. You surely didn't find Alice Gill dishonest, did you?"

"I wouldn't say that exactly, but—well, it sounds rather trifling but some of my cosmetic things did seem to get mislaid rather frequently during her last few months here—scent and face powder and so on, nothing of any real value. Of course I have no proof, but the fact remains I've had no more trouble of that kind since Alice went."

Veronica played her joker. "And yet you could hardly have given her a more glowing reference. If indeed you did write that, Mrs Garrett." She handed it over.

Mrs Garrett gave it a quick glance and nodded with palpable embarrassment. "Yes, I did write it. I wanted to be fair to the girl, after all she had been with me quite a long time and I had nothing definite to hold against her. To be charitable, that footman might not have been the chief attraction, it could be that she was anxious to better herself and it would have been on my conscience if she'd failed to get accepted because I'd given her a reference that was—well, rather less enthusiastic."

"I see. You were being kind." Veronica rose. "If I might now have a word with the rest of your staff." And as Mrs Garrett pressed her bell. "How many of them were here with Alice?"

"Just the two. My cook Mrs Berridge and Hetty, the one who let you in. The little girl Elsie is the one who came after Alice left." And in case she had caught a look of surprise at the fewness of those below stairs, "Good servants are so difficult to come by these days, and with our son away at school my husband and I find that the three of them are really quite sufficient for our needs . . . Oh, Hetty, this young police lady wants you and Cook to answer a few questions about Alice who used to be here. Alice has disappeared and they think she may have been murdered or something."

Veronica hoped she had suppressed her start. She smiled indulgently. "Oh, I'm sure it's nothing so serious. We get dozens of girls missing every week. Nearly all of them turn up quite safe, they simply felt like a change and acted on impulse. But once we get a report we have to make the necessary inquiries." She thanked Mrs Garrett and followed Hetty down perilously narrow stairs to the basement kitchen.

Hetty was middle-aged and grim-faced, undoubtedly the soul of enforced respectability. Mrs Berridge, fat and jolly, came as a welcome contrast. Neither bothered to draw Veronica's attention to Elsie, a skinny adolescent with lank hair and spots who had never known Alice Gill and knew her place well enough to contribute only giggles to the ensuing conversation.

"Our Alice gone missing?" the cook echoed with relish. "Then I reckon all you've got to look for is a pair of missing trousers. What about her Fred the footman? Has he gone too?"

"Frank," prompted Hetty.

"That's right—Frank," Mrs Berridge agreed. "I should've remembered, Christ knows we heard enough about him."

"Do you know his other name?" Veronica asked as Hetty drew in a disapproving breath at the blasphemy.

"Don't know as she ever told us that. Did she, Het? Your memory's better'n mine."

"Can't say she did."

A footman called Frank . . . This at least was progress. "I believe she met him at the Servants' Ball," Veronica said.

"At the Albert Hall," Mrs Berridge nodded. "The master

brought home tickets for us all, but my dancing days are over and Hetty here spends more time on her knees than her tootsies. It's fancy dress, Alice went as Cinderella."

"Before the ball," Hetty put in.

"All in tatters, that came easy—we tore up an old brown dress of Hetty's that she had no more use for. It was a shame really, her upstairs has got two or three fancy costumes, but the idea of loaning one to the under housemaid . . . " The cook went into impersonation to the accompaniment of piercing mirth from Elsie. "My dear, I couldn't ever wear it again. They do *perspire* so!"

"But on the whole she was kind to Alice, wasn't she?" Veronica pressed. And following a pregnant silence, "She gave her a wonderful reference."

"Seen that, have you?" The cook's chins began to shake. "She was an artful one, our Alice. No shame at all, boasted about it. Give us a real good laugh—isn't that right, Hetty?"

"It was disgraceful," Hetty said, confirming Veronica's doubt whether she had ever had a good laugh in her life.

"What was so disgraceful?"

Hetty showed no inclination to talk about it, but Mrs Berridge was ready enough to oblige.

"It was naughty of her, I won't deny that, but then we aren't slaves, are we? A girl in service has the same right as anyone else to make a move if that's what she wants. Alice wouldn't have been kept here all that time if she hadn't deserved a good character, and for Madam to refuse it—well, that wasn't so far off blackmail, was it? So I don't reckon you can blame the girl all that much for giving her some of her own medicine back."

"She threatened Mrs Garrett?"

A laughing nod. "Soon made her change her tune! Said unless she got that character she'd tell the master what their precious son had been up to last time he was home from school. The master's a very strict man, highly proper, she knew it'd upset him all right. And young Desmond being such a mother's boy— oh, there's no flies on Alice."

"What age is Desmond?"

"Sixteen, seventeen. Old enough to be accused of indecent assault."

"There was nothing in it," Hetty said.

"You saw him smack her bum, you told me. That time she was plugging in the Hoover."

"Just his idea of a joke, that was. Not very nice but I'm sure Master Desmond didn't mean any harm."

"We don't know what else he got up to, do we? For him to act as familiar as that . . . " She turned back to Veronica. "Anyway his mother wasn't taking no chances, he was due home again soon for the Christmas holidays and the very idea of her precious boy getting up to hanky-panky with a domestic servant . . . Alice got her character all right and off she went the very next day. You don't think maybe the Prince of Wales smacked her bum and Queen Mary has sent her packing?"

Hetty frowned, Elsie shrieked and Mrs Berridge quivered hugely.

9

One of the ironies of detective work is that two separate avenues of inquiry will sometimes emphasize wastage of time and effort by independently producing the same piece of sought-after information. At about the time when Veronica Knight learned of Alice's affair with a footman named Frank, a chance remark from one of those he was questioning enabled Harry Bennett to identify the man.

The break came in the third of his afternoon's interviews, the first two having given him little of any value. He had first questioned Ellen Carter, the head housemaid. Tall, square-jawed and almost male-voiced, Miss Carter was perhaps 40: a battleaxe in the forging. Her disapproval of Alice Gill, noticeable from the start of their talk, turned out very soon to be due to Alice's tiresomeness in dying at such a time. Harry gave her a reproachful look. Was Miss Carter not saddened rather than merely put out by the tragedy?

She relented but little. "One naturally feels the death of somebody one's been acquainted with, but I didn't know the girl well enough to become personal about it. I am responsible for twenty-six housemaids and if I have any favourites I try not to show it. Gill was certainly not one of them. She was apt to be cheeky but did her work reasonably well and that was all I cared about."

It struck Harry that such callous indifference might conceivably come from a rebuffed lesbian, though if Miss Carter were one he would put her down as not active or even unconscious of the fact. (The degree of innocence in the 1930s was such as to make that more than possible.) Ellen Carter, he decided, was one who liked to speak the unvarnished truth and was thus indulging herself now. All the same he'd instruct Veronica Knight to lend a special ear to gossip about her.

Miss Ethel Currie, lady's maid to the Marchioness of Wittlesham, was the garrulous little woman who had seen Alice Gill being removed by the stretcher bearers. The two sets of rooms nearest the Old Library were occupied by Ladies of the Bedchamber during their two-week spells of attendance on the Queen, and Harry was anxious to find out tactfully what they or their maids might have heard or seen between 6 p.m. and midnight.

Miss Currie frowned as though irked by the paucity of what she was able to tell him. "I don't think we can help you there, we spent very little time last night in this part of the Palace. My lady doesn't start in attendance until Her Majesty gets here today. I saw her into her apartment here at about half-past six, then I unpacked and changed her for dinner—she was dining out with the Marquess. His lordship came to call for her just before eight and it was after eleven o'clock when she rang for me to see her to bed."

"Where did you spend the evening, Miss Currie?"

"I had my supper and then went to listen to the wireless in Mrs Holloway's room. She's one of the two assistant housekeepers, a very nice lady, I like her a lot better than that starchy Mrs Wells, so I couldn't have been anywhere near the library when poor Alice had her fall. What do you want to know all this for anyway?"

"The Coroner has to be given a full report on exactly when and how the girl came to have her accident."

"I was told she died in the ambulance. I hope that's right? I saw her, you know, being carried out. I wouldn't like to think she'd already gone when I looked at her, I don't like looking at dead people, gives me the shivers."

"She was still alive then," Harry assured her, thanking his stars he wasn't superstitious or his fingers would soon get themselves permanently crossed. "Could I perhaps have a word now with the Marchioness?"

Miss Currie frowned again. "There's nothing my lady can tell you that I haven't. The two of us were together all the time until she left with his lordship."

"You said she rang for you on her return. That means she was alone in this part till you rejoined her."

"That would only be for a very few minutes. I'll ask her if you like whether she met anyone on her way in."

"Thank you, but I'd prefer to ask her myself."

Not popular. "Well, she's not here now. Their Majesties have just returned from Windsor and my lady is with the Queen."

"When will it be convenient for me to speak to her?"

"It's quite out of the question for the next few hours. She will be in attendance until Lady Ruxford takes over this afternoon, and she certainly won't want to be troubled while she's resting."

"Is being a Lady-in-Waiting so very tiring?"

"It involves a great deal of responsibility. Quite apart from that, for a lady in her position to be questioned by the police is so—so sordid."

"That's just too bad. What time does her relief go on the job?"

"Really! Her *relief* . . . " Miss Currie was as satisfactorily outraged as he had intended her to be.

"Oh never mind. I shall be having a word in a minute with Lady Ruxford and her maid. I hope I shall find them more ready to assist me." He added, "You may tell your mistress I shall be back this afternoon to speak to her."

He moved along the corridor to the Countess of Ruxford's apartment. The woman who answered his knock was dressed like Miss Currie in the accepted jersey, skirt and cardigan of the lady's maid. Miss Lucy Grant was younger than her contemporary and Harry was not surprised to find her preferable: a fair, plumpish, capable-looking woman with a rosy complexion that came as he rightly guessed from a country upbringing. Once more he mendaciously explained the purpose of his visit.

"A dreadful business," Miss Grant said. "I'm afraid we can't be of much help, though. I'll ask her ladyship if she heard anything, but we didn't arrive here from Suffolk till nearly seven o'clock and my lady said she would dress herself for dinner while I went along to their town house. It's not very far—in Grosvenor Place—and she wanted me to get a diamond clasp out of the safe there. It was a present to her from the Queen on her fiftieth birthday, and as she was going to be in attendance today she naturally wanted to wear it. I kept it with me till she rang me in my room at about half-past ten to say she was ready for bed. I certainly didn't see or hear anything unusual."

"I believe you were indirectly responsible for the girl being found?"

"That's right. I found the ashes of last night's fire still in the grate, so I rang Mrs Wells. That's when they realized poor Alice was missing. It was a great shock to me when I heard what had happened, I knew Alice Gill rather better than most of the house-maids. We had a mutual friend, one of the footmen here—Frank Craddock."

Harry wished she could have rattled on long enough to allow him a considered response to this unexpected benefit. A slight pause for a hastily summoned cough and he asked, "Have you spoken to Craddock since the accident?"

Miss Grant shook her head. "This is a very busy time for us. A visit to the Duke of Connaught at Clarence House and then these Indian princes coming here to pay homage, and after that a visit to the Duke and Duchess of Kent . . . The Queen is so energetic herself, my lady and I don't get much time to relax when we're attending."

The woman is revelling in all this, Harry told himself. Under-standable perhaps for one in her position, yet her snobbishness was tempered by her readiness to tell of her friendship with a mere footman.

"As a matter of fact I haven't spoken to Frank for some time," Miss Grant was continuing. "Just the occasional nod when we see each other here. I'd ask Alice now and then how they were getting on together because she'd told me they were walking out—and I may be imagining it but I did get the impression that things have been cooling off a little between them lately. Still, I'm sure Frank will be very upset over her death. I really must try to get him aside for a few words of sympathy."

"You knew Frank Craddock before he joined the Palace staff?" Harry ventured.

"All my life," she said. "We come from the same village—Bredenham in Suffolk. Of course he's a few years younger than me. I'm twenty-nine, so Frank must be twenty-three, twenty-four."

Harry was surprised, he had put her down as around thirty-five—probably because she gave the impression of having finally settled for spinsterdom. But even at twenty-nine surely too old to be considered as a past rival to Alice even if she might also have resigned herself to being supplanted.

"It was through her ladyship and me that he came to be a footman here. As you know they have to match, and Frank being the right height—six foot three—it was a fine opportunity for him."

"How long has he been here?"

"I'd say about two years. Alice wasn't his first girl—oh, not by any means! Such a good-looking boy, he's always had his pick. But with Alice it did look like becoming regular and that's why I was surprised when she sounded a bit offhanded the last time I asked her about him."

"Surprised or relieved? I gather she wasn't everybody's favourite."

A thoughtful pause: "Well, I wouldn't like to say anything against her now, not after what's happened. She did rather strike me as the flighty sort, I could see her leading Frank a bit of a dance. But it was really no concern of mine, and—"

The door opened. "Oh you're here, Lucy—thank the Lord, I need you—" The Countess of Ruxford checked abruptly at the sight of Harry.

Miss Grant said quickly, "This is a sergeant of police, my lady—he's making inquiries about that poor girl who was killed in the library." She turned back to Harry. "I'm afraid I've forgotten your name . . . "

"Detective Sergeant Bennett, your ladyship. I'm here on behalf of the Coroner. We're anxious to pinpoint the time of the girl's accident. She lay there all night without apparently recovering consciousness."

"So I was told. Very unfortunate."

Lady Ruxford had been a beauty as a debutante and in her fifties was still a handsome woman: tall with intelligent face and luxuriant black hair, her figure virtually unchanged since she had made her curtsy to King Edward VII. The arrogance of the well-born rich, in her voice and manner, came to her so naturally that her credulity would have been strained had anyone presumed to tell her it made her seem officious.

"I was wondering," Harry said, "if either you or Miss Grant remembered hearing the girl going to the library or the crash when she fell. As far as we can tell it would be some time between seven and ten."

"I heard nothing." Her ladyship was looking at him pointedly. "I fail to see why it should matter. What difference does it make when she fell? You surely don't suspect foul play?"

"Heavens, no." It came out over-emphatically. He moderated the smile that was perhaps making too light of the idea. "But in this job one takes nothing for granted. The Coroner insists there mustn't be the slightest room for doubt that death was purely accidental."

"I see."

"And that involves also making inquiries about the girl's private life and background." He was anxious to get back to Frank Craddock. "I understand she was keeping company with a footman here who is known to your ladyship."

Miss Grant said, "I told him it was through you, my lady, that Frank Craddock was taken on the staff."

"At your suggestion, Lucy, don't be modest about it . . . Yes, Sergeant, he was originally in our employ at Bredenham Hall. A nice lad, though perhaps a little too handsome for his own good. But far too gentle, I'd say, to go pushing girls off ladders."

A better controlled smile: "I'm glad to hear it."

"And now I have to turn you out," Lady Ruxford said. "A busy evening ahead and I'm already pushed for time."

Harry thanked the two women and left. He would have been disturbed if he had remained outside to eavesdrop while Lucy

Grant was changing her mistress for the evening attendance.

"What else has he been asking you, Lucy?"

"No more than he asked you, my lady. Could I help with the report he had to make—what time Alice had her fall and how it might have happened. I told him I wasn't in these rooms more than a few minutes last night and I certainly didn't notice anything unusual."

"But how did Frank Craddock's name come up?"

"Oh, that. I just happened to mention I knew Alice through her going out with a chap from Bredenham who worked here now."

"Have you any idea why that should interest him as much as it seems to have done?"

"He told you that himself, my lady. How they wanted to know all about Alice and her friends and what kind of girl she was and so on."

"Didn't it occur to you to wonder why?"

"I thought it was like he said: when somebody gets killed in a place like this they have to make extra sure there wasn't anybody else to blame."

"And you think they *are* quite sure about that?"

Lucy Grant turned sharply from the open wardrobe. "Don't you, my lady?"

"I accepted it to begin with as all part of routine—which generally involves a great deal of utterly pointless labour—up to the moment when I casually mentioned the possibility of foul play. It struck me then that the man—what was his name?"

"Detective Sergeant Bennett."

"It struck me that he was rather over-reacting. It set me wondering."

Lucy stared at her mistress wide-eyed. "You think Alice was *murdered*?"

"Now don't jump to conclusions, but it did cross my mind. In the circumstances they'd naturally want to keep it secret, so don't you dare breathe a word outside this room. You understand, Lucy? I have simply been thinking aloud, this conversation is strictly confidential between us."

Lucy said offendedly, "No need to tell me that, in all these years with your ladyship I never once betrayed a confidence."

"I know, I know, I'm only stressing it because in this case it really is terribly important."

Lucy caught her breath. "Oh, my God—if you're right I've done an awful thing to poor Frank. They'll be suspecting him now, won't they?"

"Calm down, Lucy, I may be completely wrong. And if I'm not it's probably a good thing you did mention him. The police would soon have found out anyway about Frank and Alice, and they'd have been all the more suspicious if they'd thought you were hiding that particular titbit."

The order was obeyed as usual: Lucy calmed herself. "You don't think our Frank could have done a thing like that, do you, my lady?"

"I'd say it's most unlikely. Though you did once consider him a bit of a menace, didn't you, Lucy?"

"That was different, I never thought he'd actually hurt Jean— at least not deliberately."

Three years ago Jean Grant, Lucy's younger sister, had become stillroom maid at Bredenham Hall, the Earl of Ruxford's seat in Suffolk. Their father had long been the village constable, a widower who had brought up four children since his wife's death when Lucy, the eldest, was 13 and Jean only 3. Their father himself dropped dead from a heart attack while on a cycle beat a few months after Jean had joined her big sister—by now Lady Ruxford's personal maid—at the Hall. Their brothers, both lucky enough to be in work at a time when jobs were eagerly coveted, had left home for the towns, and Lucy found herself more than ever under compulsion to serve as a stand-in parent to Jean.

Frank Craddock was third footman at the Hall. The only son of a local blacksmith whose wife had survived a scandal or two in the past, he was an impressive young man of towering height, well-proportioned figure and features that were conventionally prepossessing, if without great character, under fair curly hair. He was of cheerful disposition and conscientious in the performance of his duties; but he was a randy fellow more than ready to capitalize on his appeal to the girls—and, it was rumoured, more than one married woman—of Bredenham and district.

When the prettiest housemaid at the Hall suffered a miscarriage and left under a cloud, it was to Frank Craddock that fingers were pointed—whether or not with justification nobody knew for sure. Among the staff Jean Grant of the stillroom was rated even prettier and at sixteen was an impressionable girl who had more than once been caught in dalliance with Frank.

Lucy voiced her fears for her sister's chastity to her mistress, who had recently been appointed Lady of the Bedchamber. Frank Craddock being fortunately of the right height for the Palace's ranks of matching footmen, Lady Ruxford had a word with Briən Goodship and the transfer was duly arranged. Frank himself was allowed little say in the matter, the news that the Palace Steward had put in a special request for him to join the Royal Household being accompanied by the congratulations of Lord Ruxford and her ladyship on an honour which he would naturally accept with alacrity. It left him a pound or two the poorer but there was no evidence that he regretted the move. His splendid figure was enhanced by his scarlet tails, blue knee-breeches and white stockings; and he was no doubt well satisfied to find himself employed where maidservants were numbered in dozens. If young Jean suffered any heartache it wasn't for long: she was now happily married to a farmer's son from Bungay and was expecting their first in August.

"Frank never means to do anyone harm," Lucy said. "It's just that he's ruled by his heart more than his head."

Lady Ruxford smiled but restrained herself from comment: it was all too easy to shock her prim maid.

10

Superintendent Sidney Gardner, bodyguard to King George V and chief of police at Buckingham Palace, was a burly man with a rock-like face and restless eyes, as alert for danger without showing it as a road-using London pigeon. Having seen Their Majesties safely back from Windsor, he had repaired to his rooms and ordered a belated meal to be served to him there, satisfied that a routine check-up with his chief inspector could wait until he had eaten. It was a surprise to him when a knock at his door was followed by the entry of Botterell rather than the expected stewards' room boy.

"Hallo, Bob. You look worried. Trouble?"

"Too mild a word for it," Botterell said. And proceeded to give his chief a detailed account of those events since early this morning that were too confidential to be communicated by telephone.

There was a long silence after he had finished. Superintendent Gardner looked as though he was finding it hard to accept that anything so heinous could have taken place in his absence.

"Bloody hell," he said at last, quietly but with a wealth of expression.

"I hope, sir, you approve of what we've had to do."

"Wouldn't matter much if I didn't," Gardner said resignedly. "And who am I to fault Bill Roe? No, I can't really see how you could all have done anything different. But a detective sergeant taking on a job like this . . . Takes a bit of swallowing. I'd better meet the lad."

Harry Bennett, summoned to the rooms of the King's bodyguard in the late afternoon, shared Botterell's uncertainty as to whether Gardner was relieved to have had the affair taken out of his busy hands or resentful at having been unavoidably bypassed. At the Superintendent's request he reported his activities to date. Nothing was said till he was summarizing his interview with Miss Ethel Currie. Gardner's first comment when it came was totally unexpected.

"Lord Wittlesham called at the Palace for his wife?"

"That's right, sir."

"Got the time he was here?"

Harry referred to his notes. "According to Miss Currie it was just before eight."

"Interesting. Strike you that way, Chief Inspector?"

"I can't say it does." Botterell was looking as puzzled as Harry.

Gardner grinned. "You don't get my opportunities of course for picking up servants' hall gossip. I'm sure it's only a coincidence but the noble Marquess of Wittlesham has a well-known hobby—housemaids."

"You don't say!"

"I've heard complaints in more than one house on our travels. Nothing serious, mind—just the odd spot of flashing and fumbling. Bit of a joke really. And he's quite an old dear—the last sort, I'd say, who'd go in for bopping one of his fancies." The Superintendent turned to Harry. "Spoken to him yet, have you?"

"No, sir. Only to Lady Wittlesham."

Harry had returned as promised to see her in the last half-hour. The Marchioness of Wittlesham was a white-haired lady with an expansive bosom and the face of an amiable horse. She had confounded her maid's forebodings by showing a cheerful willingness to co-operate with him to the best of her ability, which was limited in that she had nothing whatever to tell him.

"No matter," Gardner said affably. "You'll agree all the same he'll have to be questioned. Like me to do it? I've always got on pretty well with the old boy."

Harry accepted gratefully.

"Carry on then." And when Harry came to the end of his report, "So at this moment the footman Craddock is just about your only lead."

"Yes, sir—if it can be called that. I want if possible to find out his movements yesterday evening, but it's a tricky business—I daren't risk arousing any suspicions."

"We might be able to help you there," Gardner said. And to Botterell, jerking a thumb towards a pile of papers on his desk. "Hand me over the week's roster, I think it's that one on top." He studied it for a moment. "Yes, I thought I noticed it. Craddock starts today as close waiter."

"Meaning he's number one King's man," Botterell explained. "Totally committed to the wants of H.M. through H.M.'s page. And in case you don't know it, a page here is what would be called a butler elsewhere."

"Close waiter means he'll be at it from this morning till nearly midnight," Gardner went on. "Even longer tomorrow, now the King's in residence. So we can assume he'd have been allowed at least a half-day off yesterday." And to Botterell, "Who did we have on the Trade Gate?"

"I'll have to check up on that, but I think it was Squires."

"He's pretty dependable. Ask him if he remembers seeing

Craddock go out and come in. If so, when."

"Do the staff have to book in and out?" Harry inquired.

Botterell shook his head. "It's fairly informal. Servants come and go as they please. Provided they're on the spot when required nobody cares much what they do with themselves. There's a porter on duty at the Trade Gate—which is the staff entrance—as well as one of our uniformed men. They pride themselves on knowing all the four hundred who work here— resident and outside, that is."

"You'd better see to it they add Sergeant Bennett to their collection," Gardner said. And to Harry, "Where do you live, Sergeant?"

"I have a bed-sitter, sir, across the river in Battersea, but I was going to ask Mr Goodship if he could find me accommodation here in the Palace."

Gardner said to Botterell, "Find out from Goodship if there's a horse-box available."

Harry blinked and Botterell translated again for his benefit. "The horse-boxes are what the footmen call their dormitory."

"With reason," Gardner said. "It's a dark, bare, miserable place, but it'll give you a chance to look through Craddock's belongings if you fancy him at all seriously. Signs of bloodstains or their removal."

Harry said, "I'd like to have a chat with Craddock, sir, if I can get him alone."

"Of course. I'll be keeping a watchful eye on the lad and I'll get in touch with you through the Chief Inspector here when Craddock has a convenient break."

It was time for Harry to report back to Scotland Yard. He arrived at Deputy Commander Roe's office as Veronica Knight was concluding her own report. Harry greeted her by her first name and was corrected by Roe. "She's Vera from now on."

Veronica alias Vera recapitulated the details of her visits to Alice's family and previous employer, then Harry told of his own findings till interrupted by the telephone.

Roe answered it, listened without comment, gave a brief acknowledgement and turned back to them.

"Autopsy report: Alice Gill was three to four months pregnant."

11

Even for those who know London intimately the familiar can have its mysteries. Never in the hundreds of times she had passed by Buckingham Palace had Veronica noticed or given a thought to its servants' entrance. As W.P.C. Knight she felt foolish at being reduced to asking directions from a constable at one of the Palace gates; but for Vera Knight the new housemaid, with scanty belongings in a cardboard suitcase, it was only to be expected. "Good luck, dear," said that future colleague from Chief Inspector Botterell's section as she set about finding her way in.

The staff entrance in Buckingham Gate was guarded by another uniformed policeman and, in a glass-fronted cubbyhole, a liveried porter resembling a top-hatted tortoise.

"Yes?" A word that can cover a variety of intonations; the tortoise's was in the aggressive category. Veronica handed him the introductory papers supplied to her, at the same time giving her new name. He studied them as if suspicious of a forgery, then reluctantly called, "Boy!"

His call had to be irritably repeated before it was answered at shuffling gait by one patently his senior, a small wizened veteran with bandy legs and arms of simian length. "New housemaid," grunted the porter as if resentful at being disturbed in surely one of the least demanding of sedentary jobs. "Take her to Mrs Wells."

"This way, girl." No offer to help her with her case.

"When do boys and girls grow up at this place?" Veronica inquired as she followed her guide along a dark, stone-paved corridor.

"There's boys 'ere older'n what I am," the veteran assured her. "Pages too. I'm an 'all boy, see? All us 'all boys is boys, same as we don't 'ave no page boys 'cause all the pages are men."

By the time Veronica had worked this out they were mounting stone steps which gave way to lino-covered stairs that took them to the third floor. The old man was able to shuffle at a quite remarkable speed and Veronica's suitcase felt as though it had doubled in weight as she puffed after him down another lengthy corridor till at last to her relief he stopped and rapped on a door.

"Who is it?" An imperious voice, but the hall boy opened the door before answering the question, "New 'ousemaid."

Mrs Wells sat over a tray of tea. She did not invite Veronica to sit down after the door had closed. Veronica quietly put down her case and stood before the assistant housekeeper as humbly as the housemaid she now was.

"Vera Knight. Is that correct?"

Veronica nodded. "That is to be my name here."

"You will call me madam."

"Of course, madam. I'm sorry."

Mrs Wells said, "I am fully aware of who you are, Knight, but while you are here you will naturally expect to be treated the same as any other housemaid."

"Yes, madam." She resents me, Veronica thought, perhaps as the only other female accepted into the male world of those in the know.

"Where was your last place? Others will be asking you that, so you'd better try it out on me."

"I was four years with a Mrs Gurney in a village near Canterbury—madam. She died a few weeks ago and Mrs Hunt's agency told me of this vacancy when I called there today. I was given to understand it had to be filled at once, so I packed and brought my things along in case I was found suitable." This was not wholly untrue: a rich, elderly Mrs Gurney had indeed died recently in the Kent village where Veronica's parents still lived.

"According to the instructions I have been given," Mrs Wells said, "your only departure from routine work will be the necessity for you to report here, in this room, to exchange notes with your fellow police officer."

"At two in the afternoon and ten at night," Veronica agreed. "I hope you won't be too inconvenienced by that, madam?"

"I shall be, of course. But I hope it won't be for long. It's not very pleasant to know one is living under the same roof as a murderer."

"I am sure the Royal Family would echo your sentiments if they knew," Veronica said tartly. And to forestall any rebuke, "I've also been told that if anything urgent comes up between those times I must regard you, madam, as the contact to bring us together."

"That is so. Now as to the arrangements: you will be taking Alice Gill's place as nearly as possible in all respects. That means you will sleep in the dead girl's bed with Clara Watson as your companion. You will take on all the duties that Gill would have done if she had still been with us. Have you any idea how a housemaid does her work? It would reflect on me if you were to show your ignorance in front of the others."

Stay humble, Veronica told herself firmly. "We never had any servants in my home," she said, "and one of my sisters is in domestic service." Poor Godetia!—a most superior nanny. "I don't think there are many household tasks I haven't tackled."

A dubious nod. "In that case I will get the head housemaid to take you in hand and run through your duties. Her name is Ellen Carter and I hardly need to tell you she has no idea of why you have been engaged. Try to make sure you give her every satisfaction, I don't want her coming to me complaining I have chosen a maid who isn't up to her work."

Harry Bennett had warned her about Ellen Carter. "A possible if not a probable. Myself I'd lay ten to one against, but I still put her in the running. You could do worse than give her a chance to make a pass at you."

Veronica took his meaning as Miss Carter conducted her first to a linen room for bedding and uniforms, then to the dismal little room she was to share with Clara Watson. A formidable type over-endowed with male hormones, but the head housemaid indulged in no giveaway glance of physical appraisal, not even to register disinterest. Veronica was left however in little doubt that Ellen Carter was a bully, such was her enjoyment of dispelling any notion that housemaids had it easy at Buckingham Palace.

"You will get up in time to be washed and dressed by a quarter past six—and I mean washed properly, I don't tolerate any young person whose body offends my nose. You will do that of course before leaving your room, hot water is a luxury only on bath nights. There are then grates to be cleared and fires laid and lit in bedrooms and sitting-rooms. You will be responsible this week for the apartments of two Ladies-in-Waiting: Lady Wittlesham and Lady Ruxford. When the weather gets warmer you may be excused the fire laying, that will depend on the wishes of your ladies.

"Curtains have to be drawn back, shutters opened where there are any. There's morning tea to be carried in, then jugs of hot water: you'll find no built-in wash basins here, the King believes it's unhealthy to sleep in a room with a waste-plug. Once you've done all that you will put on a clean apron and have your breakfast.

"You are allowed half an hour for breakfast, and—as I advise all my girls—to clear your bowels for the day. Sweeping, dusting and bedmaking come next—mattresses here are turned daily. As soon as bedrooms are vacated wash basins and chamber pots have to be emptied. There are two sittings for lunch. You will attend the first one at eleven forty-five and stand quietly in your place until grace has been said.

"You will then change into your black dress with frilly apron and cap, keeping yourself available during the afternoon in case you are rung for. In the evening there are curtains to be drawn, beds folded down and basins emptied again. Supper is taken at six-thirty and you will be in your bedroom by ten o'clock. I turn out all lights from the passage at ten-thirty."

Veronica thought back ruefully to her relief that morning when told she was not going to be asked to parade the streets again.

"I hope you are not superstitious?" the head housemaid inquired as Veronica lowered her armful of bedding to the thin undulating mattress deemed sufficient for the exhausted. There was no mistaking the anticipatory smirk.

"Not particularly," Veronica said. "Why, Miss Carter?"

"You haven't been told about Alice Gill?"

Veronica shook her head: ignorance was often useful in attracting confidences. "Who's she?"

"The girl who last slept in this bed. She died this morning."

"Oh, no—how awful! What did she die of?"

"Nothing infectious, you don't need to worry on that score. They reckon she fell off a ladder in the Old Library. Had a thin skull apparently, knocked herself out and never came round."

"What a terrible thing!" And apprehensively, "Do we have to climb ladders in this job? I'm no good on heights."

"No need if you do your work properly," Miss Carter said. "There's special brushes here with long handles that Gill ought to have been using to dust up high when she last did that room. Too lazy to bother, I reckon—and then seeing a cobweb I wouldn't miss the next time I looked in there, up she climbs to get at it. Nobody knows for sure of course, but I'd say that's what happened. You'll be doing the Old Library now you're taking Gill's place, so make sure you take the right sort of brush there. The other girl on that section is Daisy Brett. You can come down as you are now and meet her and Clara Watson, the one you'll be sharing this room with."

"Vera" Knight was excused work on this, her first evening, which she spent mainly in the company of Clara and Daisy. She found Clara no improvement on the dull, heavy girl Harry had prepared her for. Daisy was a likeable extrovert, a small cheerful Cockney who was clearly a favourite of the servants' hall, judging by her exchanges of bawdy repartee with some of the younger men as they filed in for supper.

They all went to their places at the eight long tables in accordance with the nature of their work: one table for housemaids, the next for maintenance men, others for laundry maids, porters and kitchen personnel, the sexes completely segregated. The top table was that of the scarlet-coated footmen, highest in precedence at this gathering.

"The pugs take their meals in the stewards' room," Daisy explained.

"Pugs?"

"That's what we call the upper servants, don't ask me why— the stewards and pages and under-pages and yeomen of the court . . . Sh!"

A young, fair, extremely good-looking footman was rapping on the table with a spoon. All chatter ceased.

"For what we are about to receive may the Lord make us truly thankful. The King, the Queen, members of the Royal Family, God bless them."

Another burst of chatter as all seated themselves, the footmen throwing their scarlet coat-tails back over their shoulders to prevent them from creasing.

"Quite a ceremony," Veronica remarked.

"Ceremony—that?" Daisy laughed. "Plain to see you've never worked in a big house before."

"True enough. Only six of us at my last place."

"You should have been where I was—Lord Brasted's place in Kent. Forty-three of us there, all to look after one old bachelor—and that's not counting the seventeen gardeners. Talk about ceremony at mealtimes! Us lower servants have to stand to attention at the back of our chairs, then an odd man rings a handbell and the pugs troop in, arm in arm, all in strict order of importance: butler and housekeeper, valet and cook, so on down the line—with any senior servants who happen to be visiting.

"The butler gives a signal and we all sit down to the first course, which has to be eaten in silence. Not one bloody word from anyone, just a few smothered giggles 'cause we're all trying to make each other laugh. Soon as that course is over, up get the pugs and off they go to their parlour for the next one, still careful to keep in the right order. Later they'll have their coffee in the housekeeper's room. All that as often as not for cold mutton and boiled cabbage! Too many of us here of course for that kind of nonsense, and the grub's a lot better, I'll say that for this place."

Her dismal sleeping quarters had prepared Veronica for a fresh ordeal at table and she was indeed pleasantly surprised by the size and quality of the rump steak and two vegetables served to them by hall boys, among whom she recognized her ancient guide of the late afternoon.

"Who was the chap that said grace?" Veronica had a hunch that the answer was going to give her a lucky break.

She was right. "That's Frank Craddock."

"Is he top footman? He looks so young."

"No, it's just that he's top of the roster this week. Means for one week he's the King's own footman, so he has the honour. Fancy him, do you?"

"Daresay I could. He's very handsome."

"Well, there might be a vacancy there. Anyone tell you about the girl whose place you've taken?"

"Yes, Miss Carter did. Very sad. Was she his girl?"

"He took her out a few times. But then he wasn't the only one." And Veronica intercepted a mischievous glance at the taciturn Clara that brought unmistakable hate for a brief moment to the normally expressionless face. It confirmed what Harry Bennett had already told her about Clara's feelings towards Alice. There was clearly more here than ordinary dislike.

Alone with Clara as the two of them prepared for bed, Veronica returned cautiously to the subject of the dead girl. "Clara, I'd like us to be friends but I rather get the feeling you resent me being here. Were you very fond of your other room mate? It's not my fault I've been sent to take her place."

"I don't want to talk about her."

"I'm sorry."

Clara pulled a petticoat over her head and swung round. "But don't you go thinking it's 'cause I miss her. I just don't want to think about her ever again. Got what she deserved, she did, the dirty thieving little cow."

"Oh . . . I got it all wrong then."

"Yes, Vera, you did an' all. You might be all right, I reckon— but I don't know you yet, do I? I liked Alice well enough our first night together, it's easy to be mistaken. And now I'll ask you to shut up, 'cause I'm going to thank God for paying her out like I asked Him to."

Veronica was in bed by the time she rose from her knees. "Don't you say your prayers?"

"Not since I was little."

"Same as her. Still, you didn't laugh at me saying mine, that's something in your favour. She did. Used to pinch me bum while I was talking to God, the wicked little bitch."

"You really did hate her, didn't you, Clara?"

"I had reason to. And I don't want to talk about her, I've told you that once, so shut up and good night." Bedsprings creaked under her bulk. Perfect timing: a click from the corridor and their light went out. Within minutes Clara was snoring.

Tired after what seemed two or three days' duties crammed into one, Veronica ought soon to have done likewise, but reflections on her evening, added to the bumpiness of her thin mattress and the gnawing of a mouse behind the wainscoting—the so-tough Veronica abominated mice, which according to Daisy infested Buckingham Palace—prevented her from closing her eyes for sleep till an hour or more had passed.

She wondered if Harry Bennett hadn't been a little too ready to write off Clara Watson as a suspect. True, it was difficult to imagine a moron like that beating Harry in a game of bluff but the girl was certainly powerful enough physically to deal out the described blows, and one word dropped by her this evening suggested a motive beyond hatred of a tormentor. "Dirty *thieving* little cow," Clara had said. Since Alice Gill was known to have been surprisingly well off for a girl of her circumstances, what could she have thought worth filching from Clara? A man, conceivably—but in spite of her experience of male quirkiness Veronica couldn't see any man being attracted by the snoring lump in the next bed.

That she was wrong about this, though on the mark in her other reasoning, was divulged by Daisy Brett early next morning. "How'd you get on with Holy Clara?" Daisy inquired as she and Veronica set out with their paraphernalia for the distant apartments of the Ladies-in-Waiting.

Veronica grinned. "Afraid I'm in disgrace. Got into bed last night without having a word with the Almighty."

"But you didn't mock her?"

"I wouldn't do that. She's a hefty one, probably packs a punch."

Daisy laughed. "You're dead right! Alice found that out."

"They came to blows?"

Daisy nodded. "Poor old Clara, you can't blame her. Alice did her real dirt. You'd think it hard for Clara to get herself a bloke, wouldn't you?"

"I certainly would."

"You never can tell. Me, mind, I'd go all goosey if her feller so much as touched me. Ugliest little sod you ever saw, face like a monkey, teeth all broken and black, bandy legs—forty if he's a day. But I s'pose if you've never had a bit you'll take anything."

"Sounds quite a catch! Work here, does he?"

"One of the window cleaners. They count as staff. With three or four thousand windows to keep 'em busy they never go anywhere else. Anyway, he starts courting fat old Clara, they go out together, I don't doubt they have the odd bunk-up—the uglier they are, the randier they get, that's my experience. Then Alice finds out. She and Clara had just had another up-and-a-downer, I don't know what that one was about but it must have been real vicious for Alice to do what she did. Made a dead set at Sam Riley if you please—that's Clara's window cleaner. Cruellest thing she could've done to the poor cow. With a pretty girl like Alice ready to open her legs to him old Clara never got another look-in. Sheer revenge, that's all it was, the nastiest bitchiest thing Alice could think of. Meself I dunno how she could bring herself to go through with it—'cept if a bloke had a big enough dooberry, that was all Alice cared about. But she paid for it right enough! My God, she did!"

"What do you mean, Daisy? That surely had nothing to do with her accident?" Veronica had to restrain an eagerness surpassing mere curiosity.

"In a way it did. There's something else I could tell you . . . I promised her I'd never breathe a word, but now she's dead it can't matter no more." Daisy lowered her voice. "Later." She put a finger to her lips and pointed to the door they had reached after their long burdensome walk; a scuttle of coal had been left outside it by a coal porter, humblest of ranks in the Palace servants' table of precedence. "Lady Ruxford's," Daisy whispered. "Fire in sitting-room only. Know how to lay for top lighting, do you?"

Veronica shook her head. "I've always built mine on screwed-up paper and kindling."

"Oh, that won't do for Ellen Carter. Fires here have to be lit from the top. I'll come in and show you."

"It's going to make you late, Daisy." Veronica was only too conscious of the forbidding schedule ahead of them.

"I'll manage. Not so much to do this morning—they've closed up the Old Library till after the inquest."

She lifted the scuttle, softly opened the door and went in on tiptoe, Veronica following with scoop, brush and shovel. The tone of slumbrous breathing from the adjoining bedroom remained constant. A lady's maid evidently enjoyed the privilege of later rising, for there was no sign of Miss Lucy Grant while Veronica took in her first lesson as a Royal housemaid.

"Once the grate is clean we lay a thick paper grounding to cover it, then pile up small pieces of coal with a few big lumps in front. It's only after that we put on your sticks and screwed-up paper . . . Let's have those cinders back, we use them to top it all, with just one or two more little pieces of coal. Now we light it at the top . . . There, see? Lights up right away. This fire spreads down, not up. It'll go on burning all day now, hardly needs any more attention. Saves trouble, saves coal. That's the word you hear more often than any other at this place—save, save, save. Maybe they haven't told the King the slump's over—or he might be hard up, poor old chap. Not as you'd think it though, would you? Two hundred to dinner some nights and a footman to every four of 'em."

Daisy tiptoed out. Veronica cleaned up the grate and left with the remaining ashes. Daisy had forgotten to tell her where these were to be dumped, but a friendly soul in the nearest house-maids' pantry took them off her while she put her equipment aside, washed her hands and prepared a tray of early morning tea.

Lucy Grant was coming out of the dressing-room, an evening dress over her arm, as Veronica returned with the tray to Lady Ruxford's apartment. "Ah, there you are." The lady's maid's tone suggested she had been kept impatiently waiting. She put the dress down on a chair, took the tray. "Her ladyship isn't yet awake. I'll take that in. Your fire is out."

Veronica was not altogether surprised; she had mistrusted the method from the start, though perhaps Daisy had hurried it this morning on her behalf.

She realized she had left matches behind in her housemaid's box. A hurried search of the sitting-room, no matches to be seen. She went down on her knees before the grate and set about trying to breathe life into a glowing ember. She was so pre-occupied with her task that she failed to hear the door softly open and turned only when a husky voice said, "Alice . . . "

The visitor was a young girl in a grey fur coat, windblown dark hair edging a round face with large blue eyes and a provocative if slightly petulant mouth; a washed-out look in the unsympa-thetic light of early morning was insufficient to rob it of its immature prettiness.

She caught her breath as Veronica faced her. "Oh, it's not Alice."

"I'm Vera, Miss."

"Hullo, Vera. You're new in here, aren't you? It's usually Alice who looks after my mother."

"She's no longer with us, Miss." Veronica was aware that Lady Ruxford's daughter was presumably also titled but considered ignorance on the part of a new maid to be more in character.

"Why? Where's she gone?" the girl demanded.

"She died."

"Died!" The large blue eyes grew larger, the mouth stayed open. "How? What happened?"

"I was told she fell off a ladder while she was dusting up high."

"How absolutely frightful! Are you sure?"

Veronica was still of an age to appreciate how shocking the death of a contemporary is to the young. Before she could reply Miss Grant came out of her mistress's bedroom.

Lucy Grant exclaimed, "Lady Rosalie! What *are* you doing up at this hour?"

"Haven't been to bed yet," Lady Rosalie said, opening her fur coat to reveal a shimmering pale green evening dress. "I was at the Godfrey-Bassets' dance, then some of us went on to the Embassy Club and we finished up with eggs and bacon at Lyons' Corner House. Lucy, I've just heard about Alice being dead."

"That's right, she had an accident. Lady Rosalie, you ought to be in bed. What are you doing here? I've only just woken her ladyship up."

"I've got to see her—and I want to ask you a favour, Lucy dear. Would you be an angel and go along to the Glenisters' house in Curzon Street and pack up my things and take them along to Number Ninety-six?"

Lady Ruxford came out of the bedroom, pale blue peignoir over matching nightdress. "Rosalie! What in heaven's name—?"

Veronica, back on her knees in front of the grate, was having little success with her glowing ember but was quietly enjoying this diversion, her presence either overlooked or ignored as being of no matter.

"She's been up all night," Lucy reported disapprovingly.

"But why come here?" Lady Ruxford demanded. "And what's

all this nonsense about taking your things to the house?"

"I want to go and sleep there, Mummy. Cicely and I have had the most God-awful row. I want nothing more to do with that bloody little cow."

"Rosalie, I won't have you using that kind of language! Even if you and Cicely aren't on speaking terms you can't be so rude to her parents. It's they who've been good enough to put you up while I'm in attendance here."

"Only for the last two nights—and I bet they won't even notice I've gone. Not till they get my b-and-b letter."

"But you can't go to our house without giving the Hendersons proper notice. Nobody has slept there in the last three months. The beds won't be aired."

"That won't worry me, I'll sleep in this coat if you like—and Mrs Henderson can easily rustle me up a meal before my hair appointment. Please, Mummy, do let me—it'll mean going to an hotel otherwise, I'd sooner die than go back to that foul little Cicely's place."

Her goal, Veronica presumed, was the family's little-used town house; but she was denied the result of the altercation when Lucy Grant seemed to become suddenly aware that she was still with them.

"On your way, girl. Leave that, I'll see to it."

Veronica rose. "I'm sorry, it's not the way I'm used to building fires."

Miss Grant said stiffly, "You'll have to learn a lot of new ways if you want to stay here for any length of time."

God forbid, Veronica said to herself as she took her leave with mother and daughter wrangling on. It gave her a titbit of gossip for Daisy Brett's delectation when the two were reunited after breakfast for joint bedmaking.

"She's a one, that young Rosalie," Daisy chuckled. "Not as I know her like Alice did. Proper little tart, so Alice said."

"Sounds a case of the pot calling the kettle black," Veronica commented. "And talking of Alice, there was something else you were going to tell me about her."

Daisy hesitated. "I don't know as I ought to really, but—well, it can't do no harm now. And I'd rather let it out to you, Vera, seeing as you never knew her, than somebody that did. I'd like to get it off my chest, you see 'cause I feel kind of guilty about something I said to her, like as if I was partly responsible for what happened." Another brief hesitation. "Alice was in the pudding club."

"Go on!" Again came the need to stimulate surprise; would-be detectives, Veronica reflected, could do with a term or two at drama school.

"Missed her last two periods," Daisy went on. "She'd tried all the usual ways to bring it on but they hadn't done no good, and I asked her if she'd tried jumping off a chair 'cause I've got a cousin who once brought on a miscarriage doing it that way. Alice said she'd done that all right and it didn't work, but I've been wondering ever since if she tried it again off that ladder, 'cause if she did I'd have to blame myself for putting her up to it."

"That's nonsense, Daisy," Veronica said with genuine concern for the girl's unease. "If she'd already tried the same sort of thing with a chair it didn't take you to give her the idea."

But you've just given *us* one, bless you . . .

Veronica reproached herself for not thinking of it. The investigation of such a possibility must surely help to avert suspicion of a murder that must never be publicly so labelled.

12

Inspector Charles Calkin settled himself in the corner of an empty first-class compartment and lit his pipe as the train pulled out of Liverpool Street, enjoying the rare experience of plain clothes duty and the change from taking on chores he had thought to be long behind him. At last however he was departing on a mission worthy of his rank in this strangest of all cases.

Deputy Commander Roe was anxious for an officer to visit the Suffolk village of Bredenham and find out what he could about Frank Craddock. Unable to spare Harry Bennett and limited in his choice of others, Roe had considered making the journey himself but soon realized its unwisdom. The most likely source of information was Bredenham's village constable, one P.C.

Thomas Free, who would undoubtedly smell a hulk-load of rats were he to be visited by someone of Roe's rank and reputation. But a plain inspector was appropriate to the cover story that Calkin was taking with him: a girl in his manor had been raped and strangled; Craddock was one of several men known to have associated with her; there was no reason to suspect the Palace footman but the constable would appreciate the necessity of making sure that he had no past history of violence.

The journey to Bredenham took three hours: two and a half by rail to the ancient town of Beccles, then half an hour by bus. It was the first time Charles Calkin had been out of London since he and his wife spent a fortnight at Bournemouth last summer and on this fine spring day it was a delight to look out at pleasant English countryside bedecked for the Silver Jubilee, villages and hamlets seemingly striving to make up for their lack of size with the loyalty of their showing.

Bredenham itself was no exception: a village with a population of little more than four hundred, its single shopping street so festooned with banners and bunting that Calkin found it diffi-cult to follow directions to Constable Free's house, proclaimed by the simple notice POLICE on a blue and white enamel plate over the front door.

Tom Free was a genial man in his early forties. Thinning red hair and a bristling red moustache gave him a striking resem-blance to Deputy Commander Roe, so many grades above him, and Calkin had to suppress a smile at the thought of their meet-ing had Roe been sitting where he was now. The Frees had been warned by telephone of his coming in time for Mrs Free to prepare a steak and kidney pudding with fresh vegetables from their small back garden. "We were sure you'd arrive hungry, sir, after that long ride from London"—he might have covered the distance on horseback. While the stout amiable woman pottered busily about her kitchen the two men sat with mugs of beer in the little-used front room.

As the immediate successor to Lucy Grant's father Tom Free had lived in Bredenham for sixteen years, though not himself a native of the place—he came from Lowestoft. He was also excep-tional in that he was not connected with the Ruxford estate, as were, directly or indirectly, some four-fifths of the local people.

Bredenham Hall, seat of the Earls of Ruxford since the late eighteenth century, was considered on the modest side by the standards of the time. The staff at the Hall numbered thirty-six, exclusive of fifteen gardeners. The family also had its London house in Grosvenor Place, though this was something of a white elephant these days, its only occupants for most of the year being a married couple acting as caretakers. Lady Ruxford stayed at a Royal residence when in attendance on the Queen. Her husband ventured away from Bredenham as seldom as possible. Their only son, Gerald, Lord Swaine, was a subaltern in the Cold-stream Guards at present posted to Gibraltar. His seventeen-year-old sister Lady Rosalie Carpender had until recently been at a finishing school in Paris but had come home for the Jubilee.

The seventh Earl of Ruxford was allowed scant enjoyment of his wealth. The Second Battle of Ypres had left him with a head still peppered with shrapnel after a dozen or more operations and a badly scarred face about which he was unduly sensitive. "People are used to it by now and he's a decent man. Got a terrible temper, though, and it don't take much to make him lose his rag. Not that you can blame him, they say the poor gentleman counts himself lucky when he isn't walking about with a blinding headache." The Constable topped up the Inspector's mug of beer. "However, sir, I'm sure his Lordship isn't the man you've come to see me about. The wife took the message, said they didn't give his name, but I reckon I can guess it. Frank Craddock?"

Calkin was surprised and said so.

"Perhaps I didn't ought to have jumped to it like that," Free said apologetically. "I wouldn't want you to get a wrong impression of the boy. The thing is, we live in a very small and close community and it's not often anyone here goes off to work in London. I don't think in fact it's happened at all since Frank left, so I didn't have to be a Sherlock Holmes to name him. I hope the boy isn't in bad trouble?"

"Probably not in trouble at all," Calkin said. He gave the concocted reason for his visit, suffering the same twinges of conscience as his colleagues in London over the need to lie so shamefully to trusting people. "He apparently picked this girl up in St James's Park two or three weeks ago and they met a couple of times since. Had sex in a parked car that some bloody fool had left unlocked. As far as we can gather she was only an enthusiastic amateur who didn't apparently fancy the last of her admirers. It's evident she put up a fight before he raped her and strangled her, the night before last in the deep doorway of a shop. She'd told the girl she shared a room with about Craddock being a footman at Buckingham Palace. He was off duty at the time she was killed and the shop isn't very far from the Palace, so it's theoretically possible for him to have done it, but I can't frankly see any motive—seeing that he'd already found her nicely available—unless of course he has homicidal tendencies."

There! Not a bad story: he'd made it up himself and Roe had endorsed it at their meeting last night. They had hesitated over the decision to strangle their victim rather than batter her to death but had finally settled for it as being, paradoxically, more likely and not so close to the truth.

"The first part I can believe," Tom Free said, "but not the rest of it. Young Frank always did go for a bit of skirt, and there was plenty round these parts willing to oblige. Some of our menfolk breathed a lot easier, I can tell you, when he packed up and went off to London. But I never had any trouble with him. And an act of violence—against a woman, too—no, sir, that just isn't Frank Craddock's style."

"Nothing of the sort when he was living here?"

"The opposite, I'd say. Meaning he had plenty of cause to put up his fists now and then, but I never heard tell he actually got into a fight. Bit of a cissie in some ways, Frank is. No good at games in spite of his size and strength. I remember once with the football team: our regular goalie was hurt and we talked Frank into taking his place. I was in the team then, playing left back. We was up against Ditchingham and they weren't all that good, but they booted ten goals past Frank. I don't think he made one save. I'd yell for him to come out when their forwards broke through, but he never would. Too scared of getting a kick where it mattered, I reckon. There was some nasty things said to him in the dressing-room afterwards, but it was like water off a duck's back: he just shrugged and grinned. Same with cricket, he was a real duffer. Didn't make him very popular with the other lads, specially as he was best at the one game they all wanted to be good at!" Free chuckled appreciatively.

"Any idea how he got on at the Hall?"

"Same story there, I think: O.K. with the girls, not much of a favourite with the other men. Frank Craddock's mother used to work there—laundry maid—till she married Joe Craddock, he's our blacksmith. Ugly fat bugger, Joe is, and his wife being small but pretty there's a few wonders who might actually be responsible for handsome Frank. But you'd best ask the wife about that, she worked in the kitchens up at the Hall. Before Frank's time of course, but she still keeps up with a few of her old friends there."

Over a lavish and delicious meal Mrs Free confirmed her husband's testimony. "Wouldn't hurt a fly, that boy wouldn't, not knowingly. But a devil for the girls! Takes after his mother there—she could never resist the other sex. But a nice polite boy, always ready to lend a hand without being asked. I like him."

"See what I mean?" Free winked at Calkin.

"Don't be silly, Tom, I'm old enough meself to be his ma. It's the young girls that fall for Frank. I've heard it said even Lady Rosalie's been known to make eyes at him, but that's probably just gossip. In a little place like this, sir, with not much in the way of entertainment, people like to work up a nice piece of scandal out of next to nothing."

"I understand Lady Ruxford's maid is one of his friends," Calkin said.

"Lucy Grant? Well, they know each other of course, both working at the Hall and then at Buckingham Palace, but I don't know as I'd say they were on friendly terms. Lucy's a lot older and a sight too superior for the likes of Frank."

"A snob," Free put in.

"That's right. You wouldn't believe it, sir, the snobbishness that goes on in a servants' hall. Far more than you ever get with the gentry. You wouldn't find a lady's maid like Lucy Grant getting intimate with a footman, even one that serves the King. Now her young sister, that was different. Jean Grant was said to be sweet on Frank when they were both up at the Hall together, but then one of the other maids he'd been out with got herself in the family way and I think that scared Jean off him. She's married now, gone to live near Bungay."

"Was it ever proved that he was the father of that child?"

"There wasn't a child, the girl was lucky. Had a miscarriage. Lost her job at the Hall and then married one of the gardeners there. He could have been the one responsible, but it was Frank that people put it down to at the time. I tell you, sir, there's no end to the gossip and scandal in a little place like Bredenham. But as for strangling some poor girl he'd picked up in the park—oh, never! Not Frank Craddock, I guarantee that."

With which Inspector Calkin decided he'd better rest content. The Frees had known Frank Craddock most of his life, were clearly wise to village goings-on, and by virtue of Tom's job were unprejudiced. It was doubtful whether any further inquiries locally would give him more without provoking that gossip and scandal of which Mrs Free had unconsciously warned him. He had not perhaps achieved a great deal towards the solving of this momentous murder case, but it had provided him with a rare treat of a day.

13

Frank Craddock required no alarm clock to wake and be up by 6 a.m. The distinction of being for one week the King's own footman impressed itself sufficiently on his subconscious to ensure an eager readiness for a working day that would appal any trade union leader.

Frank loved his work at the Palace. He was well aware that he cut a fine figure in the uniform he was now putting on; but pride in his physical appearance came secondary to the sense of importance that reached its zenith once in every three months. Pitched at fifteen into the kitchens of Bredenham Hall, he had long chafed under what he believed to be the ignominy of domestic service: a feeling that had remained even after his promotion to third footman in the house of a noble earl. But to serve the King-Emperor, to be actually responsible for satisfying his personal wants, that was very different, it was a job that carried to Frank's mind as much prestige as a commission in one of His Majesty's crack regiments. With luck, and provided he managed to keep a clean record sheet, he could wind up one day as the King's page—or even achieve the glory of the sergeant-footman, a being so superior to the rest of the staff that he had to take his meals alone in his office.

Frank had never ceased to be grateful to Lady Ruxford for her generosity in parting with him on learning of a vacancy in the ranks of Palace footmen. At that time the family's town house was still in regular use, and by happy chance Frank's first outside mission was to escort her ladyship on the box of the carriage bringing her from Grosvenor Place to take up attendance on the Queen. Some of the footmen disliked outside duty, entailing as it did a conspicuous walk along the pavement to the Royal Mews in scarlet splendour, with highly polished top-boots and cockaded top hat; but to be temporarily a sightseers' attraction was for Frank Craddock a gratifying experience.

And how he had been put through it that first time! The coachman beside whom he had to perch was old Joe Peach, a celebrated character of the Royal Mews with a reputation as the bane of new young footmen. Talking while riding on the box of a Royal carriage was strictly forbidden; but over the years old Joe had acquired the ventriloquist's talent of speaking without visibly moving his lips, which he employed to tell outrageous anecdotes designed to put a strain on his companion's ability to keep the prescribed straight face.

"I'll never forget my first time as Royal coachman. In the last reign, that was. Mr Robinson, their usual coachman, was off sick and I was chosen to take his place.

"That morning I had to drive Queen Alexandra. 'Where's Robinson?' she wants to know. 'He's not very well, Your Majesty,' I shouts, her being hard of hearing.

" 'What's the matter with him?' "

"Well, it wasn't the kind of thing I could bawl out, so I reckon I went a bit pink and I sez, 'I'd rather not say, Your Majesty.' She gave a tactful nod. 'I quite understand,' she sez and gets in.

"That afternoon it's the King's turn with the carriage. 'What's this about Robinson?' he asks. 'Not well, Your Majesty.'

" 'I know that. What is it exactly?'

"I goes all pink again and sez the same as before: 'I'd rather not say, Your Majesty.'

"'Don't be a fool, man,' he sez. 'You can tell me.' So I has to come out with it. 'He has a very painful attack of piles.'

"'Is that all?' roars the King. 'Then who the hell's been telling the Queen he's got clap?'"

And after Frank had seen the Countess of Ruxford into the carriage, tucked the rug round her—("How nice you look, Frank!")—and climbed back to his place on the box:

"Lucky for you, my lad, it's not old Bella we've got in the shafts. Never drove a sweeter-tempered mare, but we had to retire her. Couldn't hold her wind in her old age.

"I mind the time I was driving dear old Princess Louise. She's just stepping into the carriage when Bella lets go with the most thundering great fart you ever did hear. Bloody near blew the poor lady clean off her feet. It's so bad I feel I has to make some sort of apology. 'I do beg your pardon, Your Royal Highness,' I sez, all red and embarrassed.

"The Princess gives me the kindest smile. 'Don't worry about it, Peach,' she sez. 'As a matter of fact I thought it was the horse.'"

Frank was later to learn that both tales had long been part of Buck House folklore.

There were no windows to the footmen's 'horse boxes', situated high under the Palace roof but at least each tiny, barely furnished cubicle had its own light switch. Dressed this morning with particular care, Frank inspected himself in the speckled mirror and awarded his reflection an approving nod: scarlet tail-coat without crease, black trousers pressed to perfection, gold-embroidered black waistcoat satisfactorily spotless, stiff white shirt and wing collar freshly laundered, white bow tie a fraction out of symmetry to show it was not the frowned-on made-up kind.

As befitted the day's close waiter, he was first out of the stalls, unaware that a Scotland Yard detective with a special interest in him was concluding a fitful sleep in a neighbouring box, certainly not dreaming that this day of distinction was to turn sour on him by evening.

At five minutes to seven he entered the coffee room to fetch His Majesty's early morning tea, which with exact regularity was being set down on his calling tray as Frank came through the door. The King's valet came out of the Royal Bedroom Suite to receive it from him at precisely 7 a.m. Punctuality was in Royal eyes the supreme virtue, a view so impressed on the staff that Buckingham Palace could be said to be run almost literally by clockwork.

By the time Frank had collected and taken up the Royal mail and the day's newspapers, the calling tray was ready to be removed and cleared. Frank had a hurried breakfast in the servants' hall and went to collect dessert for the Royal Dining Room in case either of Their Majesties cared to take fruit with their breakfast. Dessert was the special responsibility of the King's footman; it was seldom touched at this hour but there would be trouble if it was not available.

At five minutes to nine Frank Craddock took up his position outside the Royal Dining Room. A footman had always to be present while Their Majesties were eating but was under strict orders to remain out of view. Standing behind the requisite screen by the open door, he was able to listen to most of the conversation though unseen by the speaker. The King's deep, gravelly voice could now and then be picked up to some advantage.

Royal servants are today required to sign an undertaking not to recount their experiences for publication. Those employed at Buckingham Palace in 1935 were under no such obligation, and one of the senior pages had long been collecting material for a book he was planning to write after his retirement. A footman who brought him a usable contribution was rewarded with cigarettes according to his estimate of its worth.

"If I had my way—" was a favourite expression of the King-Emperor, and Frank Craddock had kept surreptitiously alert for this opening. His Majesty's intentions if he had his way ranged from the taxing of foxhounds to a doubling of the Navy Estimates and were usually worth a few Woodbines.

One icy winter's morning the Duke of Gloucester complained that the cold had kept him awake in the night. "A man who is cold in bed," declared the King, "is either a fool or dead." That had been worth twenty Players.

Today as usual the King and Queen made their appearance on the stroke of nine, the King carrying his pet parrot on his arm. It was a disappointingly taciturn bird. Perched on the back of a chair, it confined itself to occasional squawking, at which the King would irritably order his page to, "Put a napkin on that damned bird's head." On one memorable occasion, however— Frank wished he had been there—the bird for no apparent reason suddenly screamed 'Shit!' In the page's presence Queen Mary tactfully affected deafness, but for once it was no cliché to say that the King laughed heartily.

Breakfast over and the Royal Dining Room vacated, Frank cleared the dessert, returned it to the kitchen and took up his morning duty at the King's door opposite the Royal Waiting Room, ready to answer immediately a ring from the blue-coated King's page and to admit His Majesty's visitors—who would have been either flattered or pained if allowed to share his knowledge of the status accorded them. A visitor in the 'minor' category was ushered into the presence by the King's page but on the arrival of a listed 'major' visitor it was the footman's duty to summon the Equerry, who would keep him company in the waiting room till the King was ready to receive him, then see him through the door which the footman held open.

There was a 'major' visitor today in the rotund shape of the Maharajah of Chukapura. Frank Craddock was later to wish the fat Indian to perdition, though more than three hours were to pass before the storm of which His Highness was the indirect cause.

Frank had his midday meal, took up the luncheon dessert to the Royal Dining Room and stayed in attendance at the door in company with the under butlers responsible for the gold and silver pieces used at table. After returning the dessert dishes to the kitchen, he took up his duty again at the King's door, where he was to remain throughout the afternoon.

Shortly before three o'clock, after a 'minor' visitor had been conducted out, Mr Gathergood, the King's page, whispered that he was taking a short break and would be in the Old Library if required. It was not unusual for the page to go out for a smoke in the course of the long afternoon, but he invariably stayed closer to hand. At Frank's startled look Mr Gathergood became indulgently confidential. "That Indian prince told H.M. he thought his horse was sure to win at Newmarket this afternoon."

Frank understood. Cash betting at this time was still illegal and senior servants fond of a flutter had accounts with book-makers who could take bets within the law by telephone. Frank put a hand to his pocket. "Could you include me in for half-a-crown, sir?"

The King's page took his coin with a nod and went. Neither of them was aware that the Old Library was being kept locked during the investigations into Tuesday night's tragedy.

Frustrated, and consequently the more determined to profit by his inside information, with the race due to start in barely three minutes' time, Mr Gathergood hurried on to the room of his friend Mrs Holloway, one of the two assistant housekeepers.

It was approximately at the time when he was explaining his urgent need to use her telephone that the King's bell rang.

Frank Craddock darted to the waiting room telephone and asked for the Old Library. "Out of commission," said the operator.

The King's bell rang again. In a panic Frank hastened out to the passage. No sign of Mr Gathergood. His Majesty insisted on his page answering a summons, never a footman; yet to put His Majesty to the necessity of ringing for a third time was to Frank's mind unthinkable. Moistening his lips while his heart beat in double time, he opened the King's door and entered.

The King was at his desk studying some papers. Without looking up he said, "Bring me the—", at which moment his eye was caught by the scarlet instead of the expected blue. He turned his head, frowning. "Where's my page?"

"He had to retire for a moment, Your Majesty."

"Find him."

As if he hadn't already tried his damnedest! Frank glanced despairingly towards the door, then braced himself to essay the forbidden.

"If there is something I might bring Your Majesty—"

The King gave him a brief withering look, then turned back to his papers without a word. Frank went miserably out, recalling the celebrated legend of the maid who was sacked from the Palace for speaking to Queen Victoria: the girl had had the effrontery to tell the Queen that a red-hot coal from the fire had sprung unnoticed on to the hem of Her Majesty's dress.

He was closing the door as Mr Gathergood reappeared. The page's mouth dropped open. "What the hell—?" There was no time for explanation. Frank jerked a thumb towards the door. "He's rung twice."

His subsequent telling-off by the King's page was the more forceful because the latter was only too conscious of being mainly to blame. "If H.M. says nothing to the sergeant-footman I'll be lenient and try to forget it, but don't you ever dare presume to do my job again, lad."

The Maharajah's horse was out of the first three and for Frank Craddock the day's tribulations were not yet over. He had earlier been given his own afternoon break, so it was a surprise when Jock Mackenzie, his relief footman, came back when the King and Queen were being served their tea.

"You're to go to the police office."

"Me? Why?"

"Only a guess but I'd say it's to do with that girl who got killed. Took her out a few times, didn't you?"

"Not for weeks. Don't see how I can help them."

"Well, don't ask me. And come back as soon as they've done with you, I'm off this evening."

Which was where Jock Mackenzie was wrong. Six hours later he was collecting His Majesty's nightcap from the Royal cellars— a 'Joey' of whisky and a Brighton Seltzer—still in the dark about the reason for his unexpected tour of duty but fearing the worst for poor old Frank.

Jock Mackenzie was glad now he'd never himself given way to the temptation of dating that hot little Alice Gill. Looked like there was something real fishy about her so-called fatal accident. . . .

14

"Window cleaners . . ." The Palace Steward was studying his staff records. "Yes, here we are: Riley, Samuel. Born Belfast 1898. Came to us February 1934. Have you reason to suspect him?"

"Miss Knight has unearthed something that makes him a possible," Harry Bennett said. "He could have had a motive—and also, I suppose, the opportunity. Not, I imagine, that he'd still have been cleaning windows as late as eight o'clock."

"Don't bank on that. Our maintenance men are doing a lot of overtime this week."

"I'd like to know what time he signed off on Tuesday."

Goodship said, "You want to see old Tim Gedge, our chief window cleaner. Chief Inspector Botterell will put you in touch with him. Anything else?"

"Yes, sir. This one's a bit trickier. I'd like to question one of the footmen—Frank Craddock."

"Oh Lord—it would be that one! He's attending the King today."

"So I understand."

Frank Craddock, still smarting over his indiscretion and re-buke, was at this time on call outside the room where the informal Royal tea was in progress.

"How long will you want him for?" Goodship asked.

"Depends on what he has to tell me, sir."

"Is he a suspect too?"

"I'll know that better once I've talked to him."

Goodship sighed. "Very well, I'll have him relieved. Where do you want him?"

"Superintendent Gardner is allowing me to use his office while he's out," Harry said. "I'm going there now."

"Right, I'll send Craddock down. Try not to keep him longer than you can help, Sergeant."

Chief Inspector Botterell knew the window cleaner Sam Riley. "Ugly little bugger. Irishman. Can't say I fancy him as a killer, but you never know with that lot. We'll see what Tim Gedge has to say about him. Why are we interested, Sergeant? Better agree on our cover story."

Harry said, "I'm officially here, sir, for security purposes. Riley being Irish could be a bit of a bonus. We have to keep an eye on Ulstermen who think the grass is greener down south."

Botterell grinned. "I doubt if Sam Riley's thoughts go that far. But I agree, it's a useful cover. We'll get Tim Gedge in."

The chief window cleaner, bald, tubby and genial, was openly puzzled by their interest in Sam Riley. "Where was he working Tuesday? Let's see, it'd be on the side facing the Mall. Can't have the public spotting a dirty window on Jubilee Day. Why, what's the matter? He's not in trouble, I hope?"

Harry ignored the question. "What time did he leave here on Tuesday?"

"Have to look at me time sheets. He was on overtime, I know that."

"Go and check up," Botterell said. "But don't say anything to Riley."

"Couldn't do that anyway, guv'nor—he's off sick."

"Since when?" Harry demanded.

"Didn't come to work yesterday or today."

Sergeant and chief inspector exchanged glances. "The window cleaners live out," Botterell explained.

"Sam lives in Kilburn," Gedge added.

"Have you checked what's the matter with him?" Harry asked.

Gedge shook his head. "He'll be in tomorrow, it's pay day. If not, then it'll be three days and he'll have to send us a doctor's certificate. Time then to find out if I'll have to replace him. It's my guess he's been on the booze. Happened before around Christmas. Not been and done something stupid, has he?"

"Depends who he's been mixing with," Harry said.

"Ah, I get it!—the bloody Irish. Might plant a bomb in the State Apartments, eh?" Gedge chuckled. "If our Sam's one of that lot, then I'm Primo Carnera. Only two things he cares about—his booze and a bit of the other when he can get it. But he's not one of them rowdy Irish and he's good enough at his work, that's all as concerns me."

"Do you know his address in Kilburn?"

"Not offhand. Get it for you in a couple of ticks."

"Do that," Botterell said. "And don't forget the time sheet." And when the man had gone, "Though I doubt if that's going to help much. Easy enough for him to clock out and then sneak back into the Palace through another entrance."

"Who do we get to call on him, sir?"

"Could be the local police," Botterell said. "But it might be better if I send one of my own men."

Harry nodded. "I'd prefer that. The more we can prevent outsiders getting curious—"

"Exactly . . . Yes, Edwards?" A constable had put his head round the door.

"The footman Craddock is here, sir."

"Sergeant Bennett will see him in the Superintendent's office," Botterell said.

Harry left him and moved into the adjoining office. There was a sullen expression on the young footman's handsome face. Harry invited him to sit down.

"I'd rather stand."

"Please yourself, Craddock. I thought you must have been standing for most of the day."

"I'm used to it."

Harry went into his explanatory preamble. The news of Alice Gill's pregnancy had certainly made it easier to conceal the true purpose of his questioning. "A sudden death in the Palace has to be investigated very thoroughly indeed, as I'm sure anyone who works here will readily understand. Not because there's any suspicion of foul play but because we have to make doubly sure there wasn't."

No comment. Craddock's was a normally sunny disposition unsuited to a display of animosity, giving the impression that the young man was overplaying his resentment. A pointer to guilt or mere crassness? Harry was unsure.

"I understand you knew Alice pretty well?"

"I knew her."

"I said pretty well. Meaning intimately."

"All right, put it that way if you like."

Harry said, "Craddock, why are you so reluctant to answer me frankly? You've nothing to feel ashamed about, have you?"

This brought a little more in the way of results. "No, nothing. I'd hardly spoken to Alice this last month or two. I'm sorry she's dead, but there's been nothing between us for so long I just don't see what it's all got to do with me."

"Did you know she was pregnant?"

"Pregnant? Alice was?" For Harry's money it was genuine surprise.

"Three to four months. Could you have been responsible?"

"Yes, I—I suppose I could. We had it off a few times, I'm not denying that. But I wasn't the only one."

"Who else?"

A shrug. "Don't ask me."

"Meaning you don't know or won't say?"

"Both. Wouldn't say if I did know. Could be a mate. What does it matter anyway?"

Too dangerously near why it did matter. Harry was once more conscious of his cramping limitations when he said, "I am trying to ascertain what if anything the girl was doing about it. Did she confide in anyone? Who did she blame for it? Did she try to get rid of it?"

"Why all the bother? Won't bring her back to life."

"No—but my job is to satisfy the Coroner that nobody pushed her off that ladder in the Old Library."

"Well, if anyone did it wasn't me."

Good lad, Craddock!—you've presented me with the opening I was dodging around for. A grin. "Glad to hear it. Just to confirm that, you'd better tell me what you were doing on Tuesday evening."

"I wasn't here. Not in the Palace, it was my night off."

"Where were you then?"

"Let's see, I—yes, of course, I went to the pictures."

"Who with?"

"Nobody. I went by myself." A lie, a palpable lie; this one was no actor.

"Pity," Harry said. "Means you can't prove that."

"I could if I wanted to." The peevish expression was back. "Don't see why I have to."

Harry sighed. "Now you're being difficult again. The more you try to avoid answering my questions, Craddock, the more I wonder just what you're so anxious to hide."

"I've nothing to hide! I went to the pictures alone, like I said, but I picked up a girl there. She was alone too, we got chatting."

"Where was this? What cinema?"

"That one at Marble Arch."

"The Regal or the Pavilion?"

"The big one."

"Regal. I went there myself Monday night." Liar speaking to liar. "Good picture. You a Joan Crawford fan like me?"

"Yes, I like her fine."

Evasion right enough. It'd be just too bad if Joan Crawford *did* happen to be in whatever film was showing at the Regal.

"So that convenient pick-up of yours can confirm you were nowhere near Buckingham Palace when Alice Gill died. What's her name and where do I find her?"

"I don't know."

Incredulously, "She didn't tell you her name?"

"No. Like I said, we just had a bit of a chat."

"Nice for the people sitting round you. Or did you take her somewhere afterwards?"

"I asked her, she said she had a date."

The telephone needed answering. "Sergeant Bennett . . . Yes, sir, he is . . . Very good, sir. I will." He hung up. "Your nameless lady had a date—and walked out of your life."

"That's right."

"So we're back where we were, aren't we, Craddock? You still can't prove you weren't here in the Palace to push Alice off that ladder."

An audible catch of breath. "My God, are you telling me somebody actually did? Why couldn't she have been alone in there when it happened? Climbed up for some reason and then lost her balance."

"That is almost certainly what did happen," Harry said reassuringly. "But in this job we're paid to be suspicious of everything and everybody . . . All right, Craddock, on your way. I don't think we shall be hanging you just yet awhile."

The footman's relief at his dismissal was undisguisable; but his face fell again when Harry added, "By the way, that telephone call was from the Palace Steward. You are to report to him immediately on leaving here."

Chief Inspector Botterell had been joined next door by Super-intendent Gardner, patiently awaiting the vacation of his own office. Harry gave them a summary of his interview, adding his conviction that the footman had something to hide.

"I know the feeling," Gardner said. "Just back myself from an interesting little talk with Lord Wittlesham."

Harry's eyes opened wide. "You think he's hiding something too, sir?"

"I wouldn't go as far as that, but I don't think we can cross the old boy out completely. He said he never saw the girl, heard nothing—but to my mind he made it a shade too emphatic. Then as if on an afterthought he tried to make me feel I had no business troubling him with such a low-class matter. It wasn't a good performance, I'd say he was definitely uncomfortable. But it could be simply embarrassment. He probably knows I know his reputation as a housemaid fancier. See what D.C. Roe thinks."

"He rang through for you a few minutes ago," Botterell told Harry. "You're wanted back at Scotland Yard. They've turned up something important."

15

Tempers were rising high in the Palace Steward's office. Word had just reached Superintendent Gardner that the footman Frank Craddock had been deposed as close waiter by order of the Master of the Household. Gardner, not having been consulted, burst in on Brian Goodship with the red swelling neck that his men of the Palace police had learned to view with apprehension.

"To go and do a bloody fool thing like that without at least giving me warning . . . God damn it, I'm the one responsible for the King's safety, it should have been my decision before any-one's."

"Then go and argue it out with Sir Wilfred," Goodship said curtly. "I've only done what I was ordered to."

"You are the one who told him the man was under suspicion.

You might have guessed that doddering old idiot would start wetting his pants. Couldn't you have talked him out of it?"

"I didn't choose to, because I can see his point."

"You too, Goodship?" Gardner dealt his head a despairing punch. "Oh my God, I give up! Even if that footman did do in that housemaid—and it's still nothing more than a possibility—do you seriously imagine he's next going to brush me aside and hurl himself at the King or the Queen?"

"No, certainly not, but—"

"If that was on the cards, then you've made it far easier for him now. As the King's bodyguard I or my deputy could have kept him well under surveillance. Now I shan't know where he might be in this bloody great warren."

Goodship said impatiently, "Neither of us seriously believes there's any danger to a member of the Royal Family. But if Craddock did kill that girl and the news eventually gets out, people are going to ask why in the name of sanity we allowed a suspected murderer to be in personal attendance on His Majesty."

"And to protect your precious reputations you've gone and set tongues wagging all over the bloody Palace—the very thing we're all out to avoid."

"Don't exaggerate, Gardner. If you'll only calm down and listen to me for a moment . . . I've made it known that I consider it unfair for one particular footman to have all the glory of waiting on H.M. at this very special time, therefore during Jubilee Week those highest in seniority will share the duty. That, I think, ought to remove any suspicion that Craddock is being victimized."

"They're not going to swallow that," Gardner grunted. "Things have never been done that way before, and a change of procedure at this place is so rare it's likely to fan those rumours—"

The telephone rang. A couple of words and the Palace Steward was on his feet. "Have to leave you, the Queen wishes to see me." He went out hoping the long walk through the corridors might remove visible evidence of his exasperation.

As he could have guessed, Queen Mary was doing crochet when Lady Ruxford admitted him to the Queen's private sitting-room. She barely glanced up at the announcement of his presence.

"I have just learned that there has been a fatal accident in the Palace." Her Majesty's tone suggested that it was remiss of the Palace Steward to allow such a happening.

"I'm afraid so, ma'am. An under housemaid had a fall from a ladder."

"What in the name of goodness was a housemaid doing up a ladder?"

"It's difficult to say for certain, ma'am, but we believe she must have spotted a cobweb on one of the high shelves when she went to draw the curtains in the Old Library. She apparently climbed up to remove it—there is still evidence of it—and she must have lost her balance."

Two or three centuries ago, Goodship reflected, such flagrant lying to a king's consort would have taken him on a one-way trip to the Tower.

"A most unfortunate thing to happen at a time like this."

"It is indeed, ma'am." (May Your Majesty never discover how unfortunate it actually is!)

"Mr Goodship, I am very anxious that news of this tragedy should not reach the King. As you know, His Majesty has not been in the best of health and our Jubilee is putting a great strain on him. It would upset him, I know—as indeed it has upset me."

"We are trying to keep the incident as quiet as possible," Goodship said. "The Press have not been informed and steps are being taken to have the inquest postponed until after the main celebrations. I have the assurance of Sir Wilfred Jennings that it will be handled with the utmost discretion."

An approving nod. "I will have a word myself with Sir Wilfred."

How had the Queen found out? The self-satisfied expression of her lady-in-waiting was sufficient answer. Brian Goodship decided to venture. "I very much regret that Your Majesty has been upset by this sad event. I hoped that it might be kept quieter than it obviously has been."

The Queen said stiffly, "Mr Goodship, I have a deep concern for the welfare of my servants. Lady Ruxford was quite right to inform me of the tragedy. I wish to send a letter of sympathy to the girl's family, so you will please supply my secretary with the necessary details. And you will also instruct my treasurer to make an appropriate contribution towards the funeral expenses."

"I will see to that, ma'am."

A curt gesture of dismissal. Brian Goodship could not resist a reproachful glance at Lady Ruxford as he backed out. Entitled as he was to feel proud of the discreet manner in which this crisis had thus far been handled, he resented the Royal implication that he had somehow failed in his duty. Coming on top of Superintendent Gardner's unjustified criticism, his normally well-contained temper was under further severe strain as he strode back to his office. It would probably have erupted for once had it not been subjected to a cooling period of an hour or so before Detective Sergeant Bennett was back requesting a fresh scrutiny of the staff records, substantially more laborious this time since it called for an examination of first names.

Harry Bennett's painstaking efforts to preserve the few charred remains of Alice Gill's burnt letter had been rewarded. Comparably patient work at the Yard's laboratory in Hendon, where the salvaged fragments were photographed on an orthochromatic plate and printed on compression paper, produced traces of handwriting on two of the four. What appeared to be the right-hand side of a figure 3 or 8 was discernible on one; the other showed the capital letters LEO followed by a semi-obliterated N. To Deputy Commander Roe the likelihood that this was a signature, or part of one, made an immediate investigation essential. There was of course the possibility that the letter had been written to Alice by somebody who had no connection with Buckingham Palace; but if the revealed figure was an 8 it could have applied to a time of day. Alice Gill met her death around 8 o'clock, perhaps while keeping an appointment with the writer of the letter, who in that case was almost certainly to be found inside the Palace.

Harry's return visit with this information brought a groan from Brian Goodship. "Anyone here called Leon or Leonard . . . Means a pretty lengthy check-up. I have cards for well over a hundred male staff."

"How many female staff?"

"Oh, my God—you're surely not suggesting a woman could have done it?"

"We take nothing for granted," Harry said. "If there's a Leonora—or perhaps even a Leonie . . ."

Goodship groaned again. "All right, all right, it'll have to be done, I can see that. I'll start right away, but it's going to take time."

"I have to see Chief Inspector Botterell again, sir, if you'll kindly ring me there when you're through."

The Palace Steward nodded, already at work.

16

Chief Inspector Botterell had important news for Harry. "The man I sent to check on Sam Riley has just been through on the blower. Riley's not sick at all, he's done a bunk."

"Good God. When was this?"

"Tuesday night. He had one room in this woman's house—" Botterell consulted his notepad, "a Mrs Moir. He saw her before he left, said his father had died and he had to go back to Belfast. He was already packed and on his way out."

"Did you gather what time that was, sir?"

"I've sent P.C. Edwards back there to find out. Riley signed off here, incidentally, at 6.42 p.m. on Tuesday. And here's something rather significant, Sergeant. I've been looking up times of Belfast boat trains. There's nothing out of London after 7.25 p.m. Even if he went straight back to Kilburn from here, he couldn't possibly get himself to Euston in time."

"So why did he leave his lodgings that night instead of early next morning?"

"Exactly. I think the story of his dead father is a lot of cock. He's got some reason to disappear."

Harry said, "It's lucky for us he said his father was dead, not dying. There must be a good few Rileys in and around Belfast, but it's unlikely more than a handful will have died this week."

Botterell nodded. "You'll naturally get the Belfast police to check on that." And as his telephone rang again, "This'll be Edwards back, I hope . . . Yes, Edwards? . . . She's sure about that? . . . And he left no forwarding address? . . . Hold on a minute." He put a hand over the mouthpiece. "Riley left the house just after nine o'clock, Mrs Moir knows that because she was listening to the news on the wireless when he last spoke to her. Get Edwards to have a look round his room, shall we?"

"Yes—for security reasons of course. And tell him to find out if possible how and when Riley received the supposed news about his father. Letter—telegram—telephone message?"

Botterell was relaying this to his man in Kilburn when another constable put his head round the door to announce he had brought Tim Gedge back. Harry ordered them to wait outside.

Botterell hung up. "Edwards had already asked the woman about that. She thought he must have had the news at work. No message for him to her knowledge, and she knows there was no letter for him by the evening delivery because she picked it up herself."

Tim Gedge, brought in for the second time, had been recalled as he was leaving and had lost some of his geniality. "What now?"

Botterell said, "Why did you tell us Riley was off sick?"

"Well, he is, isn't he?"

"No, he's not. He packed up and left his lodgings Tuesday night."

"Go on!"

"Did he send you a message or telephone you to say he was sick?" Harry asked.

"No, I just took it as how he must be when he didn't come to work Wednesday. What else was I to think? When a bloke don't turn up I put him down as sick and that's that. You don't expect me to go traipsing off to where he lives and make sure he takes his nasty medicine, do you?"

Harry said, "He told his landlady his father had died and he had to go back to Belfast."

"His father!" Gedge chuckled. "That's a good 'un. Must have had one, stands to reason, but he was brought up in an orphanage. Told me that more than once. What's the silly bugger playing at?"

"That's what we want to know," Harry said. "What else do you know about him?"

"Not much. Let's see . . . Well, he was in the Army, I know that, 'cause we was both of us at Passchendaele and never got a scratch. I don't know as Sam ever went back to Ireland after he'd been demobbed, he'd been a long time in London 'fore he came to us."

"He must have brought references," Botterell said.

Gedge nodded. "I wouldn't have taken him on without 'em. I can look 'em up, but I seem to remember he come to us from one of them big window-cleaning firms . . . That's right, out Willesden way. But I still can't believe he's up to any funny business like what you've got in mind, not Sam Riley."

"We still need a reason for why he's behaving this way," Harry said. "Let's have details of those references. New jobs still aren't too easy to get, so it's just possible he might try his old employers."

Tim Gedge left them. Harry said, "I don't think we need trouble the Belfast police after all, sir."

Botterell agreed. "It's my guess he's still in London. I doubt he'll get far once you've put the Yard on to him. And if he's the bastard we're after, at least it's a relief to have him out of the Palace."

"But until we know for sure I keep on regardless," Harry said.

"Of course, Sergeant."

"I think, sir, I'd better have another word with Clara Watson. I'll make it just a coincidence that I happen to be questioning her again. Nothing to do with Alice Gill this time. She's a dull girl, I only hope she's dull enough to accept my word for it."

Clara in fact showed an almost bovine indifference at finding herself faced again by this nosey copper. "Mrs Wells said it's not about Alice, it's something else."

"That's right. You're getting quite an important person, Clara! What we call a key witness." The attempt to jolly her along was abortive: her expression, if such it could be termed, remained unchanged. "I'm told one of the window cleaners here is a friend of yours—Sam Riley."

The hint of a frown at this. "What about him?"

"He's gone missing . . . You didn't know that?" A shake of her head. "He left his lodgings on Tuesday night and hasn't been seen since. Have you any idea why he would do a thing like that?" She shook her head again. "When were you last with Sam?"

Clara shrugged. "Few days ago. Can't remember when."

"As recently as last Tuesday?"

"Could have been."

"Try to think, Clara. Have you been out with him this week?"

"No, I have not!" Spoken with emphasis. "I don't go out no more with Sam Riley, that's all over."

Harry said gently, "I don't like to pry, Clara, but would you mind telling me why it's over between you?"

Her lips tightened. "That's my business."

"Then I'll have to guess. I'd say you dropped him—and I don't blame you if I'm right—because he took up with Alice Gill."

"You said you wasn't going to talk about her," Clara reminded him accusingly.

"Sorry, so I did. Just tell me though if I'm right."

She shrugged again. "Never did fancy him much anyway. Dirty little Irish toe-rag."

"But you were still on speaking terms."

"No, we wasn't. I told him I didn't want nothing more to do with him. That was more'n a month ago now and I never have."

"You said just now you spoke to him only a few days ago."

"No, I did not! He spoke to me."

Harry suppressed a sigh. "All right, let's say you had a few words with each other. Where was this?"

"Bow Room," she said. "I was doing me dusting, he was on the windows."

"Inside or out?"

"Out. I didn't take no notice of him, then he put his head in and said hullo. I didn't answer. He tries soft-soaping me—says he's lonely, there's no other girl for him 'cept me, won't I please go out with him again. I told him I wouldn't, not ever. He starts climbing in through the window, then Mrs Percival comes along —she's the head housekeeper—and he ducks out again. That's the last time I see him."

"Well, perhaps you won't mind telling me a few more things about him. I know he's been living on his own in Kilburn, but has he got a wife or did he ever have one?"

"Not as I know. He said he wasn't married—but then he would, wouldn't he?" She tested Harry's self-control by adding, "I made it plain I don't steal other women's husbands."

"He came originally from Belfast," Harry went on. "Any idea how long he's been in England?"

"Never asked."

"Do you know if he has any relatives?"

"Never heard so."

"He didn't ever mention his father?"

"Hasn't got one."

"Oh, so you do know that."

"Only 'cause he said how he was brought up in an orphanage, same as me."

Two of the unfortunates—unattractive, unloved; this was when one counted one's blessings.

"Has he any special friends that you know of?"

"Got his mates at work, that's all I know."

"Any particular mate?"

"Not as I know."

"Can you suggest anywhere in London where we might catch up with him?" Harry asked patiently. "Not because we've got anything against him, simply because he's now on the list of missing persons and we have to make sure nothing serious has happened to him. Now please think, Clara: does he have any favourite pub or café? Is there any special place—a park, somewhere like that—where he likes to go in his leisure time?"

"Dunno." She was beginning to fidget, though more from boredom, he believed, than because his questions were bothering her.

"How many times did you go out with Sam?"

"Two or three, didn't count."

"And where did he take you?"

"He didn't take me, I had to pay for meself. He's a stingy bugger."

"Then where did you go together?"

"Pictures."

"Anywhere else?"

A shrug. "Lyons's, ABC."

"Any particular one?"

"Nearest one to the pictures."

"No pubs?"

Her lips tightened again. "I don't go to public houses."

Harry smiled. "He must have been fond of you, Clara, if he was willing to give up his beer for your sake."

"He still found plenty of time for that."

"What about religion—Catholic, is he?"

"Never asked him."

"He didn't go so far as to propose marriage?"

She shook her head, then changed her mind. "Well, sort of . . . He said he'd like to marry me only he couldn't afford it, not unless I kept on me work, and I said then we might just as well not be married 'cause I'd only get the push if they found out. Us domestic servants aren't supposed to get married, you know that. Good thing I never said yes. Married to that little sod!—I'd sooner stay single the rest of me bloomin' life."

And with that Harry Bennett decided he would have to be content. Not, he feared, that her answers would be of much help to the Yard in their search for Sam Riley.

He returned to the Palace Steward's office. Brian Goodship scowled up at him. "No use your coming back yet, I'm not halfway through."

"I'm not trying to hurry you, sir," Harry assured him. "Just looked in to say I have to go now and see D.C. Roe. The finger seems to be pointing to that window cleaner of yours." He gave Goodship a brief summary of their findings. "But naturally we still have to cover all other possibilities." His eyes went to the papers spread over the desk. "Any luck yet, sir?"

"Hardly what I'd call it," Goodship grunted. "One Leon, one Leonard. I'm not a gambling man, but I'll willingly lay you a hundred to one against either of them being your man."

"Which further shortens the odds about our new favourite," Harry said.

At Scotland Yard he enjoyed again the priority given to his case by D.C. Roe; another deputy commander and two chief inspectors glanced curiously at the detective sergeant for whom they had been politely asked to give way.

Roe listened without comment till the sergeant had delivered his latest report. "It's difficult, sir, to see Clara Watson as a *femme fatale*," Harry concluded, "but I suppose Riley's disappearance could be attributed simply to the fact that she's thrown him over."

Roe nodded thoughtfully. "Why not? One mustn't be influenced by one's personal feelings. Like sees like through different eyes. Your lumpish housemaid might be safe on a desert island with you or me, but to that gorilla of hers she could be Juliet."

"Meaning you think Romeo may have done away with himself?"

"It's on the cards. Taking the cause of his frustration with him—Alice Gill. Or he could have meant to do that, then lost his nerve when it came to his own turn. Or he could have tried to start things up again with Alice and lost his temper when he found he'd already served his purpose. At this moment his motive is secondary to the importance of finding the man—dead or alive. We'll put out a call for him right away. No reason for anyone to link him up with that girl's death, though we'll play down his last job as much as we can. Without his cards he won't find it easy to get another. Unless he's stuck in the mud at the bottom of the Thames I've no doubt we'll soon have him."

The machinery for a hue and cry was set in motion. "Take a look through these." Roe handed over a bunch of papers while telephoning his orders for the apprehension of Sam Riley. "The medical, forensic and fingerprint reports. I've got to admit I've seldom known a case that offered us less."

Harry studied them. Victim dealt four separate blows by almost certainly right-handed person. Victim's skull slightly thinner than normal—an unexpected bonus for the killer. No dust particles traceable from murder instrument, suggesting likely polished surface. (Bottle? Leg of a chair? Must ascertain what has been done with those various articles of furniture taken away for replacement lately.) No evidence of a struggle—blood on curtains and carpet of victim's own blood group. Bleeding localized—meaning presumably that the killer might have avoided being splashed.

Frank Craddock's prints matched none of those taken in the Old Library. (Which signified little: nobody would remark on the sight of a footman wearing gloves.) Samples of Riley's prints should not be difficult to obtain, but here again they would be of slight value even if repeated in the library—unless of course it could be proved that his work had never taken him to that section of the Palace, which was most unlikely.

"Pretty bleak, sir," Harry agreed as Roe replaced his telephone.

"And nothing there to indicate it's necessarily a man we're after," Roe said. "So what about Clara Watson? I know you find it hard to see her in the part, but you say she's a big hefty girl and we know how she felt about Alice. Fill me in on her."

Harry referred to the notes supplied by the Palace Steward. "She's twenty-six. Ten years in Royal service, three at Windsor Castle, the rest at Buckingham Palace. Mother was Ethel May Watson deceased, father unknown. The mother died when she was eight and she was brought up at Carswell Grange, an orphanage near Windsor. That's all I have on her background. No complaints against her at the Palace. According to Mrs Wells she's a good and conscientious worker but not very bright. Miss Knight told me she's a bit of a butt among the other servants."

"Which could make her dangerous," Roe observed. "I remember a job when I was first out of uniform: young fellow named—I forget, Reggie something or other. Fat and flabby, a few marbles missing. Good mechanic, though. Had a job in a big garage up Finchley way. Given a bad time by his workmates, then one of them is found on an allotment with his head bashed in. Nasty piece of work, hard to find anyone with a good word for him. Used to bully our Reggie more than most of them, but we couldn't bring ourselves to suspect him at all seriously. He did it, though—suddenly decided he couldn't take any more. I believe he'd have got away with it too if he hadn't come clean and told us the lot. He'd plucked up courage, you see, for once in his poor miserable life and he couldn't bear the thought of nobody ever appreciating it. He went to Broadmoor, probably still there. There may be no parallel at all in the case of Clara Watson, but it doesn't do to ignore the possibility. I think I'll have Inspector Calkin do some probing there, same as he did with Frank Craddock."

Harry said, "I wanted to have another word with you, sir,

about Craddock. There's no doubt in my mind he's hiding something. Question is: what and why? I think it's essential he's watched, and that's where we're up against it." Harry explained the difficulties of surveillance as stressed by Superintendent Gardner.

Roe had no ready solution. "He's right of course, we daren't risk having the man tailed by anyone who doesn't know the facts. We'll have to put most of our reliance here on Veronica Knight. Let her throw herself at him—she fell for him at first sight, he's got her so crazy she has no shame. Damn it, she's an attractive girl and we know how susceptible he is. Have him put on extra duties that'll keep him inside the Palace till—when's his next time off?"

"He has Sunday afternoon."

"Then tell that young woman he's not to be allowed out of her sight."

"I'll do that, sir. Superintendent Gardner asked if we'd like any letters for him to be intercepted. They go through the Palace's own post office and the staff there have had to do it before—there's the odd spot of corruption sometimes, servants taking bribes from shops or companies to stock their goods."

"Have it done then, as long as you're satisfied there's no chance of anyone smelling a rat . . . God, what a bloody handicap we're labouring under this time! May we never have another like it while I'm in the job."

Harry Bennett said, "Amen, sir."

17

"A *housemaid*?" The eyes of the deputy sergeant-footman bulged incredulously. "Do you seriously imagine I am the kind of man who could become involved with a *housemaid*?" He was an enormous man of 50 or so, sitting in his crimson and gold magnificence over an untouched meal brought to him in his office a minute ago.

"I am not suggesting any such thing," Harry assured him.

"Please try to understand my position. A royal servant has died in what was obviously a pure accident. The King's Coroner requires conclusive proof that nobody else had a hand in the tragedy. We know the girl received a note that morning from somebody named Leon or Leonard. I am under orders to question all members of the staff who have one of those names. You are, I understand, Mr Leon Blum." He smiled. "Not of course the French politician!"

A regrettable attempt at levity: a fist crashed on to the table setting the contents of the tray in cacophony.

"Don't mention that man to me! A *Socialist!*" A word plainly so loathsome as to need no qualifying adjective. "Isn't it enough I have to suffer the same name without having it thrown at me?" And overriding Harry's muttered apology, "I am an Englishman, I have no trace of French blood in me. My ancestors came from Strasbourg, seven generations of us have worked for England's kings and queens. My father was a page here before me, my grandfather was also a page, my sons will be following me here when they are old enough—I married late in life—and if God is good one of them may rise to where I am now or even to be the sergeant-footman himself if I am not to be so blessed. And you ask if a Blum has been mixing himself up with a housemaid!"

"Really I did nothing of the sort—" Harry's feeble disclaimer was lost in the torrent of indignation.

"For thirty-one years I have served Their Majesties. Even as an under-footman in the reign of King Edward VII I never lowered myself to look twice at any of the young females in the servants' hall. My wife was lady's maid to a Woman of the Bedchamber. I am now forty-nine years old, a happily married man, a successful man, a respected man. You could parade all the housemaids here in front of me and for all the notice I take of them I would not recognize one in ten."

Harry had a fleeting mental picture of the Guard being changed in the Palace forecourt from the Coldstreamers to a company of mop-bearing housemaids under the command of the deputy sergeant-footman. He apologized again for troubling that personage and made his retreat from the office in the nick of time for his self-restraint. Either the man was an actor capable of outpointing Charles Laughton or the Palace Steward had pinched the odds in rating him only a hundred to one.

The next on Mr Goodship's list was the ultimate in contrasts and, on his appearance, a far more likely candidate. Leon Krek, one of the lowly coal porters: a dark, handsome young man of 34 with a slight foreign accent, a son of Serbian refugees brought to England during the Great War.

Had he known Alice Gill? The pretty one—oh, yes indeed! So terrible a thing to happen, pretty girls ought not to die like that.

How well did he know her? Not well: he so much wished it, but for him—a deep sigh, a shake of the head—she was so very cold. Just a little word here, a little word there, no more.

Had he ever invited her out with him? No, no, never—he was not so bold. He would have no chance. A girl of her sort would not be seen out with a poor coal porter.

Harry Bennett was still not conversant enough with class distinctions at Buckingham Palace to accept such humility. Suspicion stirring, he asked, "Did you ever write her a note?"

"No, sir—not ever."

"Are you telling me the truth, Krek?"

"I swear it!"

"Then we'll have that down on paper." They were in a basement storeroom. Harry took out his notebook, laid it open on a pile of crates, held out his fountain pen. "Write I have never written to Alice Gill and sign it with both your names—Leon Krek."

There was a pause, then the young man braced himself. "Please don't ask me to do that, sir."

"I am not asking, I am ordering you to do it."

"Please, sir . . ."

"Go on, Krek! Do what I say."

"Sir, I cannot!"

The tone of despair dropped the penny. "You mean you can't read or write?"

A sorrowful gesture of admission. "I am from Serbia. My father worked on a farm, we had no school. When I come to England I am too old and too shamed to learn. In my work it makes no matter. I carry up the coals, I am very strong, I run with many dishes and never break, I wait on other servants. Who has need to read or write for that? But I beg you, sir, please you won't tell. If they find out I know what they say—You cannot write your name, you are no good to carry coals. I will be out from my job, and I have my mother to look after—she is very old, she cannot work. Be kind to me, sir—I beg you be kind."

A masterly get-out? Harry couldn't believe it: an ex-foreigner of such ingenuity would hardly have entered his thirties still a humble coal porter. But he couldn't help chiding himself for being perhaps too easily moved in dismissing Leon Krek from further consideration.

"All right, Krek, don't worry, I'll say nothing." He turned and made a quick exit, fearing an outburst of osculatory gratitude.

From the information that next on his list was the Palace 'vermin man' Harry inferred that Leonard Hobson must be Mr Goodship's other long-priced outsider. He saw no reason to change his mind after tracking Mr Hobson down to a corner of the Music Room in the first floor State Apartments. As animal lovers are sometimes said to resemble their pets, Leonard Hobson with his beady eyes, thrusting nose and sleek grey hair was a little crouching rat of a man. His prey at this moment was a mouse which had that morning abruptly terminated the piano practice of a daughter of the Chief Accountant of the Privy Purse.

"Keep you busy, do they?" A friendly approach after Harry had once again stated his identity and the false purpose of his presence.

Mr Hobson raised himself up on his knees. "Jes' had the electric put in. That's stirred 'em up an brung 'em out. Not as I'm grumbling. There's enough in this old Palace to see me through the rest of me time. What was that name you said?"

"Alice Gill."

"Never 'eard of 'er."

"The girl who was killed in an accident."

"Oh dear. Never 'eard about that either. They don't ever tell me nothing. Jes' pop this in." From an old biscuit tin he had taken a square of dampened bread which he pushed through a gap in the skirting board.

"She had a letter that morning from someone called Leonard."

"Not this one. Wife and seven kids. I should think so! There you are, me beauties. Come and take your nice bread and milk."

"What is it really?" Harry was curious.

"Like what I said, bread and milk—dosed in squill."

"Squill?"

"Squill poison. Juice of a plant they grow in them 'ot countries —Spain, Africa. Better 'n traps. Cheaper too. You'd need to spend a fortune on traps for a place like this—six 'undred and two rooms, one and an 'alf miles of corridors. Traps for that lot? Oh dear, dear."

"Do you happen to have worked in the Old Library lately?" Harry asked.

"Old Library? Let's think. No—must be six months or more since I was last there. Don't go in much for books, rats and mice don't." He was perfectly serious. "And I'll tell you something that'll surprise you: they aren't so 'ot on cheese as most people think. Or on fish or dripping. Oatmeal, tallow and bread, them's their favourites. Give 'em another piece for luck." Another square of bread went through the gap and Mr Hobson set about packing his equipment into an ancient haversack. "People 'ave some funny ideas, I don't know I'm sure where they get 'em all from. I remember young Prince 'Enry once watchin' me at work in the Throne Room. 'Oughtn't you to be wearing gloves, my man?'—Mr Hobson's impression of a posh voice. "He said he thought they wouldn't touch nothing I'd left me smell on. Load of balls I told 'Is Royal 'Ighness. They don't mind, I reckon they like the way I smell, I never 'ave no trouble catching all I can do with." He rose to what seemed little more than his kneeling height. "Well, I must be getting on. Nice of you to come and talk to me, mister—it's a lonely bloody life, this is."

Harry let him go. He had no more hope of results from the last on his list, a 16-year-old kitchen hand named Leonard Rodwell. He borrowed the head chef's office for the interview and was all the more convinced he was wasting valuable time when this Leonard came smiling in: a cheekily self-possessed youth with fair silky hair and a peach-like complexion.

"I was told you want to see me. A policeman, they said. What's poor little me supposed to have done?"

"Did you know Alice Gill?"

"The maid who was killed? I suppose I'd know her if I saw her—but I wouldn't want to see her now!"

"She received a letter from someone called Leonard just before she died. I take it that wasn't you."

"You take it right, Mister Policeman. I've never written to a girl in all my life."

Harry could believe it. He met a knowing look that turned into a conspiratorial smile . . . My God, the little bastard is *flirting* with me . . .

"Besides," the boy added, "I never use the name I was ducked in the font with. Everybody knows me as Lennie."

The door burst open to admit a stout angry man in chef's attire, tall white cap perched on spiky red hair above a florid face.

"What's going on in here?" Blazing eyes were fixed on Harry. "What are you doing to this boy?"

"Just who in hell are you?" Harry demanded.

"I am Winkelbaum. This boy works under me. I will not have him bullied."

The boy giggled. "Oh, Winkie, don't be such an old silly, he's a nice man. He only thinks I bumped off one of the housemaids."

Dangerous! Harry decided the joke was best treated as such. "A slight exaggeration. But the boy has more sense than you, Mr Winkelbaum. There are certain things I have to ask him and he is quite willingly giving me his answers. Now please leave us and allow me to get on."

Winkelbaum said obdurately, "Lennie is a minor. You have no right to treat him like this without an adult being present."

"But I don't need anyone, I'm rather enjoying it," Lennie assured him.

It had the effect of further aggravating his protector, which was probably what the wretched youth intended: the big man stepped forward and grabbed him by the arm. "Come on, out of here."

Harry thrust himself between them and pushed Winkelbaum back. "Stop that! Take your hands off him and get out of here or you'll find yourself in serious trouble."

"I don't scare so easy!"—said with defiant quivering jowl.

"Then I shall have to charge you with obstructing a police officer in the course of his duty—and that may not be the only charge either."

"What do you mean by that?"

"If you don't know you'll soon find out."

A desperate bluff. Any charge must lead to a revelation of why the boy was being questioned. Did the big man but know it he could beat this police officer to a pulp with impunity.

Eyes met eyes for two or three tense seconds, then without a word Winkelbaum swung round and stamped out. Lennie was giggling again. Harry turned back to him with an effort to mask his relief.

"All right, that'll do. I'd had all I wanted from you anyway."

"Nothing more?" A tone of mock disappointment. "Oh, well —so ends my first third degree."

Harry had to restrain himself from launching a kick at the backside of the provocative departing figure. Thank God that concluded this whole abortive venture. He'd pack in his career and apply for the dole if Alice Gill met her death at the hands of a Leon or a Leonard.

18

For his second country outing this week Inspector Charles Calkin drove himself in his own Austin Twelve to the twin towns of Windsor and Eton, where the favoured ones of the future sauntered top-hatted through beflagged streets, lending irony to the propinquity of Carswell Grange, Home for Female Orphans, in which Clara Watson had spent her formative years from eight to sixteen.

According to her card in the Palace records the Home was in Bagnall Avenue, an offshoot of the Reading road. Bagnall Avenue was little more than half a mile in length, but a slow drive to its end and back revealed neither the name nor the appearance suggested by it among the rows of compact middle-class homes.

An elderly man was coming from one of them with a bag of bowls woods. Calkin stopped his car and called out an inquiry.

"Carswell Grange?" A tone of amused surprise greeted this. "Bit late in the day, aren't you? Been gone a long time. It was burnt down."

Calkin upbraided himself for accepting the address in the

Palace records without making a check. "When was this?"

"Oh, let's see. Must be all of six or seven years. We moved here in 1930 and it was a shell then. Stood where those two new houses are." The man pointed across the road. "Orphanage, wasn't it? I did hear one of the kids set it on fire."

Clara Watson left in 1925, so at least she was free of suspicion on that one.

"I suppose you wouldn't happen to know anyone who was connected with the place?" Calkin asked.

"Afraid not. They might be able to help you at the Town Hall."

Calkin called first at the offices of the *Windsor Express*. He was supplied with a back number containing a full account of the fire, which had been more accidental than his informant had suggested: a senior girl upset a pan of fat during a cooking lesson; Carswell Grange was an old Victorian building in which the flames quickly took hold. Only the walls were left standing, though blessedly none of the occupants was hurt. This was largely due to the excellent disciplinary measures, for which credit was given to the new principal, Miss Jane Garstin.

New principal . . . So unless she had been a promoted member of the staff she would not have known Clara Watson. Nor even in that case could she have been of any help, for the same local newspaper reported her death two years later while living in retirement in Eton.

No detailed records of Carswell Grange existed at Windsor's charming old Town Hall, since it had been run by a private charity outside the council's jurisdiction; but Calkin's luck changed as he was about to take his departure.

"You were asking about Carswell Grange?" The speaker was a youngish man who had been sitting at work in the background while Calkin made his inquiry. "I don't know if this is of any use to you, but my late father was a solicitor here and he used to act for a previous principal of the Home, a Miss Bailey-Forbes. I don't know what happened to her, she may be dead by now — I don't think I ever met her myself but for some reason her name has stuck in my mind."

Which was curious because the name was vaguely familiar to Charles Calkin too. He thanked the young man and consulted the local telephone directory. No Bailey-Forbes. On the off-chance he tried the London directory. One here: Bailey-Forbes, A., 14 Gresham Court, W.2. He rang the number. No reply.

Random inquiries at some of the long-established Windsor shops having failed to put him on to anyone who had once worked at the Home for Female Orphans, Calkin drove back to London with the mortifying sense of having bungled this assignment. No policeman is infallible, but few have resented the fact more than Inspector (later Assistant Commissioner) Charles Calkin.

Bailey-Forbes . . . The name kept nagging at him. Where and in what circumstances had he come across it before?

Past Kensington High Street Calkin turned left on impulse and drove up through the park to Bayswater. Gresham Court was a large new block of luxury flats close by Lancaster Gate. Hard to imagine the ex-principal of an orphanage living in these surroundings; but the one here might conceivably be a wealthy relative able to provide a clue—if now back home.

The buzzer at No 14 was answered almost immediately by a pleasant-looking woman in perhaps her late sixties. She was still in outdoor clothes: smart, expensive clothes, Calkin noted. He introduced himself, showing his warrant card.

"I'm sorry to trouble you, I did try to telephone."

"I've only just got in," she said. "Been doing my week-end shopping. How can I help you, Inspector?"

"I am trying, madam, to trace a Miss Bailey-Forbes who was at one time a principal of Carswell Grange, an orphanage in Windsor."

"Then you have soon been successful. I am Anne Bailey-Forbes, I used to be there." She smiled at his involuntary look of gratified surprise. "Do come in." She led him to a bright and sizeable sitting-room. "I'll just take these things off and put on a kettle. We'll have some tea—unless you'd prefer something stronger?" She waved a hand towards a well-stocked drinks table.

"Thank you, tea will be fine for me."

Left alone, Calkin looked around. The best in furniture, tasteful and no doubt costly curtains and cretonnes, some nice pieces in the way of ornaments. A photograph in a silver frame caught his eye. He rose and picked it up. A middle-aged man with a

noticeable likeness to Miss Anne Bailey-Forbes; the smiling face
too was vaguely familiar.

Then he had it. Of course!—Claude Bailey-Forbes, unluckiest
of lucky people; Calkin was surprised now that it had not come to
him sooner. Must be eight or nine years ago: he'd been station
officer at Rochester Row when they'd brought the man in after
his arrest—the last of his arrests. All for the same offence: flying a
kite—or, as it would have been known in Claude Bailey-Forbes's
own circle, cashing dud cheques. An alcoholic or near it, but an
amiable one: Calkin remembered his cheerful badinage when
charged. The most memorable thing about him, though, was his
stunning mixture of good and bad luck.

For his latest offence—putting it over three or four London
hotels—Claude Bailey-Forbes was sentenced to eighteen
months. That was a week or so before Derby Day. Had he only
managed to stay honest a little while longer his money problems
would have been over, for among his listed possessions was a
Calcutta Sweepstake ticket which drew the winning horse and
netted him some £50,000. The news was broken to him in jail.
Claude Bailey-Forbes was allowed barely half a minute to relish
it before his stroke. He died without recovering consciousness.

Miss Bailey-Forbes came back into the room as Calkin was
putting the photograph down. "My brother." She smiled sadly.
"You look as though you may have known him."

He nodded. "We met briefly—not very happily, I'm afraid."

"Poor old Claude," she said. "A weak, silly fellow but I was
very fond of him."

"Nobody ought to be treated as cruelly as he was," Calkin
said.

"A dreadful thing," she agreed. "Though what he'd have been
like with all that money to fling around—" She shook her head
doubtfully. "He never married, you know. As his nearest relative it all came to me. That was how I was able to retire and settle
down here. Life can be very strange and ironical, can't it?"

"How long were you at Carswell Grange?" Calkin asked.

"Fourteen years."

"So you must have had a good many children through your
hands—and I'm afraid the one I want to ask about was probably
more forgettable than most. Clara Watson."

"Oh, I remember Clara," she said at once.

He was surprised and relieved. "You do? For any particular reason?"

"Yes indeed. Tell me, Inspector, is the girl in trouble?"

"I hope not. I'll go far enough to say I think not. This is simply a routine inquiry."

"May I know why?"

"A girl was beaten up and found unconscious—in fact she still is unconscious," Calkin said smoothly. "We believe we know the man who did it, but we also found that this girl had been stealing from Clara. In other words, Clara had a motive as well as the opportunity, so we felt it necessary to investigate her past in case there's any history of violence. That's where we thought you might be able to help."

"I see. How much do you already know of her past?"

"Not a great deal. That she's illegitimate, father unknown. Mother died when she was eight, which was when you took charge of her. At sixteen went to work as a scullery maid at Windsor Castle. Left after three years to become a housemaid on the fairly large staff of a titled family—I've been asked not to name them. She's still with them and seems to have given every satisfaction."

"Then I wouldn't have thought her earlier history would be all that important."

"A tendency to violence can lie dormant for years, then suddenly break out again—as we have good reason to know." Calkin glanced at her shrewdly. "What was it about Clara Watson that made you recall her so easily, Miss Bailey-Forbes?"

A long pause. "Excuse me, I'll get the tea." She went out thoughtfully, to come back a few minutes later with a loaded tray for which Calkin helped her to clear space on a table. "I suppose it can't do any harm to tell you now," she said. "Clara's father was far from unknown—I confess to making a false statement when I drew up her references. His name was Sidney Watson. Does that ring a bell?"

"I can't say it does."

"I'm not surprised, it was a sordid little case hardly worth reporting. He and Clara's mother were married all right. They were cat and dog, always fighting. The last time he hit her over the head with a flat-iron and killed her. The child saw it all. He was hanged and we took in little Clara. I thought it kinder to put her down as illegitimate rather than the daughter of a man who ended his life on the gallows. She was far from bright and she grew up without showing any sign that she remembered that awful experience. I must admit, though, that for such a stolid, almost lethargic child she could show a surprising turn of temper. She didn't often lose it, but when she did—oh, my! I remember once it took three of us to hold her down after she'd flown at a bigger girl who poured some ink over her hair. But she was only about ten or eleven then, and I must say in her favour that those rages became progressively rarer as she got older. I wouldn't have recommended her for that post at Windsor Castle otherwise. And if she's had a clean sheet over these last ten years I shouldn't think there's much danger now of heredity rearing its ugly head."

Except that nobody in those years was likely to have wronged Clara quite so viciously as had Alice Gill . . .

19

It was a surprise to Detective Sergeant Bennett when shortly after midday on the Friday he received a request to visit Mrs Wells at once in her sitting-room. He was due to go there in any case at 2 p.m. for one of his pre-arranged meetings with Veronica Knight, and her wish to see him earlier could certainly not be for the pleasure of his company; the assistant housekeeper had never disguised the fact that she found their use of her room an intrusion tolerable only because it was testimony of her loyalty.

Harry was aware as soon as he entered that the normally phlegmatic woman could hardly contain her eagerness to see his reaction to her news. First, though, she had to justify the revelation.

"I am about to betray a confidence, Sergeant, which is something I never thought I should be guilty of. But the circumstances are so important that I think I should be failing in my duty if I were to keep silent."

Fat chance of that, Harry mused. He said with a nod of agreement. "In a case like this, Mrs Wells, a piece of valuable information must certainly take priority over any moral scruples."

Her preamble nevertheless continued for a further minute of self-justification before she came out with it.

Miss Ethel Currie, lady's maid to the Marchioness of Wittlesham, was on friendly terms with Mrs Holloway, the other assistant housekeeper, and had confided to Mrs H. that she lied to the detective who questioned her about Alice Gill.

Far from seeing or hearing nothing of note last Tuesday evening, Miss Currie had come out of Lady Wittlesham's apartment a few minutes before Lord Wittlesham arrived to collect his wife for dinner and had seen his lordship—who had his back turned and hadn't seen her—in the act of closing the door of the Old Library. She had kept this to herself on learning of Alice's death because she was only too well aware that her master had an unfortunate weakness for young servant girls and she was naturally reluctant to involve him in an inevitable scandal.

She had no doubt of his lordship's innocence. If, as she supposed, he had followed Alice into the library, the girl had obviously not yet had her accident at the time when Miss Currie saw him coming out: he was a kind and decent man who would never have left an injured person to lie there unattended. It was this knowledge that had induced her to keep her lips hitherto sealed.

It would however have taken a stronger will than Miss Currie possessed to make nothing of this revelation. She had to part with her secret to her friend Mrs Holloway, who promised never to divulge it but found herself equally incapable of such restraint and duly passed it on to her opposite number Mrs Wells, who immediately realized it was incumbent on her—the only one of the trio who knew that Alice had been murdered—to relay it in her turn to the police.

"I am quite sure it is something your superior officers will take very seriously," Mrs Wells concluded. By now on familiar terms with three of them, she had never accepted the detective sergeant as anything more than a go-between.

Harry was conscious that on this occasion he was undoubtedly nothing more; the only question was whether Lord Wittlesham should be interrogated by Superintendent Gardner as before, or by Deputy Commander Roe, with whom he was unacquainted. Since it is easier to confess perfidy to a stranger than to its previous victim, the task went to Roe, who ascertained in a tactfully phrased telephone call that his lordship was lunching at his club. It was here that Roe found him, fortunately seated by himself in a quiet corner of the coffee room.

James Alaric Oswald George Logan, Sixth Marquess of Wittlesham, was a portly man looking older than his age of 56, three-quarters bald, with a permanently amused expression which was an accident of physiognomy, for his face seldom broke into the promised laugh; his lordship made few jokes and understood few more. Though anything but a clever man he was well respected, being gentle and considerate, with pleasantly humble manners for one born into the high aristocracy.

Death duties had not yet developed their most savage bite when he succeeded to the title in his mid-twenties and the family fortune was still of enviable size; he owned a stately home, Coverlings, in Sussex, a London house in Portman Square, and a shooting lodge in Scotland which he rented out, being opposed to blood sports—if, that is to say, one excepted the killing of butterflies, which were his main interest.

Lord Wittlesham's collection was said to be one of the finest in Europe, but few others had seen it, for it was kept hidden away at Coverlings in vast drawers in a series of specimen cabinets. Every winter he would add to it through a lepidopterous safari to India or Brazil or the West Indies. "Looking forward to some well-earned relaxation," he would say as the weather turned cold in autumn. Nobody however could divine what he needed to relax from. His estates and his town house were run impeccably, provided his lordship could be restrained from lending a helping hand; and though he was conscientious in his attendances at the House of Lords he had not spoken there since making an ass of himself in 1924, when during a debate on afforestation he rose to make a point fully covered by the previous speaker while Lord Wittlesham's mind was on his recent acquirement of an Australian Giant Skipper. He had indeed never done work of any kind, unless that could be said of his time in the Army during the Great War, when his obvious unsuitability for command gained him an early appointment as a staff officer.

But Superintendent Sidney Gardner had been right in assert-ing that the Marquess had a hobby other than butterflies. In his pre-puberty days young James had chanced upon the family's august butler being manipulated in the wine cellar by a pretty housemaid. It had made a deep and lasting impression on the lad. When the time came for him to plan the loss of his virginity he looked no further than the ranks of Coverlings housemaids for a young woman prepared to oblige him. The butler's hand-maiden had long gone but the one of his choice was willing enough, though insistent that coupling must not be allowed to take place while she was on duty. James duly met her by appoint-ment in the woods of the estate, but the eagerly anticipated event turned out a disaster. Dressed in her cheap finery, with a shud-der-inducing hat, she was so utterly devoid of her former appeal that he returned home unsatisfied and scorned, but with the consolation of believing that he had rid himself of an obsession about which he was too ashamed to talk to any of his con-temporaries.

It was a short-lived illusion. In blue or black printed uniform with cap on head and legs encased in black stockings, the younger variety of housemaid was still irresistible and had so remained. As Superintendent Gardner had said, his lordship's excesses were limited to flashing and fumbling; to be faced with a pater-nity suit by a domestic servant was a risk too dreadful to contem-plate. Many a hostess had received complaints about the behaviour of the distinguished guest, but always they had been dismissed with an indifferent shrug or an amused smile. What was the world coming to if a gentleman of Wittlesham's rank could not become playful now and then with a nubile skivvy?

Lady Wittlesham, a tolerant woman, was more amused than upset by her knowledge of his kink. Having dutifully endeav-oured to provide him with an heir, she called it a day on the arrival of their fourth successive daughter and took little interest thereafter in her husband's sexual inclinations, restricting herself to a single recommendation which he declined to accept. "I am told there is a Dr Freud practising in Vienna or somewhere who specializes in curing your sort of trouble." To which he replied that the good doctor would only attempt to ascertain its origin, of which he was already fully aware. "And if *you* have heard of the fellow he'll be famous enough to charge the earth. Ridiculous waste of money." His lordship did not add that he had long since ceased to regard it as trouble but rather a source of occasional harmless enjoyment of which he had no desire to be deprived.

Now suddenly it had become anything but harmless. For the second time in two days it had brought him into confrontation with a high-ranking policeman who plied him with awkward and embarrassing questions. And this one was a great deal more menacing that his old friend Sidney Gardner: for Deputy Commander Roe had decided on a direct attack as probably the most effective tactic.

"I am not going to apologize if my presence in your club is an embarrassment, my lord, because you have brought it on yourself by your evasions when you were questioned by my colleague."

Lord Wittlesham bridled. "That is a very offensive statement. What justification have you for making it?"

"Early on Wednesday morning a girl was found dead in the Old Library at Buckingham Palace with a severe head wound. You were told this by Superintendent Gardner and asked whether you could give him any useful information because you had been in the vicinity of the Old Library on Tuesday evening at approximately the time the girl must have met her death. You said you had nothing to tell him, but we now know that you were yourself in the library around that time."

"True—but why should I bother to mention that? My visit to the library was nothing to do with anyone else."

"Why did you go there?"

"Why?" An absurdly long pause. "I—I wanted to look somebody up in *Who's Who*. A man I thought my wife and I would be meeting that night. I thought I should know something about him."

Sharply, "What man? What's his name?"

"He's—er—he's . . . You've got me nervous, his name escapes me."

"Because you've only just invented him! Because you are lying again! You followed that maidservant into the library, didn't you? Don't try to pull any wool over *my* eyes, Lord Wittlesham, because I know damned well you did."

A guess that needed little inspiration. It duly worked. The Marquess drooped visibly in his leather-padded chair. "All right, maybe I did."

"There's no maybe about it. You followed her in to have a bit of fun with her. You surely don't imagine we are unaware of your reputation, my lord? So let us please have nothing but the truth from now on. You will only make it worse for yourself otherwise!"

A regretful nod. "I am sorry. I was only trying—rather unsuccessfully, it seems—to avert a scandal. Not so much for myself but for the sake of my poor wife. As of course you know, she is a Lady-in-Waiting to Queen Mary. I am sure anyone with gentlemanly instincts would have done the same."

"I think so too." With the admission of what Roe now felt was the truth, his aggression turned to sympathetic understanding. "And if you'll continue to be perfectly frank with me, that scandal may yet be avoided. So please tell me—in your own words, as we say, as though you could tell me in anyone else's—just exactly what happened with you and that girl on Tuesday night."

Lord Wittlesham nodded resignedly. "Very well. I called at the Palace just before eight o'clock to take my wife out to dinner. I was nearly at the door of her apartment when I saw this maid going into the Old Library. She had a nice figure, looked a pretty young thing, and—well, you say you are familiar with my little weakness. I went in after her. But I am afraid I wasn't welcome."

"I want the details."

"This is really most embarrassing . . . She started to close the door behind her, but I pushed it open again and went in. I think I said 'Hullo' and she said 'What do you want?' Not respectfully you understand, but rather boldly and rudely, not at all in the way that girls of her sort usually respond. I said something like 'What a pretty girl you are' and—and I think I touched her."

"Where did you touch her.?"

"On her breast. She didn't look the sort who would mind, but I was wrong—it made her very angry and indignant. She knocked my hand away and said something indecent."

"What did she say?"

"She said 'Get out of here, you dirty old —'" He could hardly bring himself to repeat it—"'f-u-c-k-e-r'."

"And then?"

"I took the hint and went. I have never forced my attentions on any young woman who made it plain that I was offending her."

"But there have been complaints about your behaviour."

"Only about an original approach before I realized I was making a mistake."

"You have never persisted with a young woman who repulsed you? I mean physically."

"Certainly not."

"Not even on this occasion, when it would be natural for you to lose your temper after the way she spoke to you?"

"I had my temper perfectly under control—I always have. What are you suggesting?"

"I am suggesting that you didn't give up so easily, my lord. That you grabbed hold of the girl and struggled with her, as a result of which she fell and cracked her head. That you then panicked and hurriedly made your exit."

"Leaving the poor thing lying there bleeding to death? That is monstrous! Do you seriously believe I am the kind of callous brute who could do a thing like that?"

Roe said quietly, "No, sir, I don't, but I wouldn't be doing my job properly if I was content to take your word for it . . . You were wearing a dinner jacket?"

"I was."

"How many dinner jackets do you own?"

"I think it's four. Two here, two at my place in Sussex."

"Who is your tailor?"

"Threlfall and Watts." Said as though it was naïve to think he might have any but the best.

"They made all your dinner jackets?"

"They did, but I don't see—"

"We are going to have to borrow them. That is to say, the two you have here in London. They will be examined for bloodstains —or for any attempt to remove them."

A startled protest. "My dear man, that's out of the question! My valet has charge of them. How the devil am I expected to explain a thing like that to him?"

"We are prepared to make it easy for you, my lord."

Roe had discussed the point with Gardner and Bennett. It was easy enough to take temporary possession of clothes kept by a footman in a box that would leave a pony squeezed for room; it presented a problem in the case of one who never looked after his own things. Could the Marquess but know it, they were no less anxious than he was to remove all risk of sinister gossip.

"Have you an appointment for tonight?" Roe went on.

"I have, yes. An old friend has asked me to dine with him early and then visit a theatre."

"I'm afraid you must cancel it," and disregarding a querulous frown, "now listen carefully, my lord. We have booked a room at the Savoy Hotel—at your expense, I need hardly add. You will come there at seven o'clock wearing the dinner jacket you had on the other night. One of my men will be there to receive you and take over the jacket. You will telephone your valet and tell him a waiter has had an accident with a bowl of soup, it was spilled all over you. He or one of your other servants is to bring your second dinner jacket at once to this room, which the hotel has put at your disposal while the other one is cleaned. My man will also take charge of the second jacket and rush the two of them to our forensic lab. I have made arrangements for both of them to be dealt with immediately and I am assured you will have them back within a couple of hours."

"Good heavens." Lord Wittlesham shook his head wretchedly. "What a prospect!"

"I am sorry," Roe said with scant sincerity, "but you must realize we are going to great pains to spare you further unpleasantness . . . Frankly," he added, "if it were not for your standing, and especially Lady Wittlesham's Royal appointment, I would probably have asked you to accompany me to Scotland Yard, where you would have been held until we were satisfied with your story."

A hasty acknowledgement. "Yes indeed, I do see that and I am most grateful . . . It's only knowing as I do that I am utterly and completely innocent . . ."

"Which I'm pretty damned sure the old boy is," Roe said later in giving Superintendent Gardner an account of the interrogation. "But it'll be a long time, I guess, before he grabs another housemaid by the tits!"

20

Six worried men sat in the Commissioner's office at New Scotland Yard on Saturday morning. Superintendent Gardner had joined the five who had gathered here last Wednesday, worried then, more so now. Ostensibly the meeting had been called to discuss final arrangements for the events of Monday—Jubilee Day—when the King and Queen would be driving in procession to St Paul's for a Thanksgiving Service; but since every measure had already been taken to ensure the usual smooth efficiency of these royal occasions, it was inevitable that their attention soon turned to the matter weighing most heavily on their minds.

The fact of Alice Gill's murderer being still at large was too sore a point with four of the five for the subject to be readily broached, and it was left to the Master of the King's Household, Sir Wilfred Jennings, to ask the needless question that was a gentlemanly criticism of police shortcomings.

"Anything fresh on the—er, the death of that girl?" Sir Wilfred clearly could still not bring himself to use the word 'murder' in connection with a happening at Buckingham Palace.

"It can't be long now before we catch up with your window cleaner," the Commissioner said with determined confidence. "I'm frankly surprised it's taken as long as this to find him." A reproachful glance passed the buck to the Assistant Commissioner who was head of the C.I.D.

"We don't yet know if he's the man we really want," the A.C. observed.

"And it's beginning to look to me as though he may not be," Deputy Commander Roe said. "If he's innocent he won't know we're out for him, so he won't be taking any evasive action. It's the ones who are looking over their shoulders all the time who are the easiest to spot."

Sir Wilfred said unhappily, "So if Riley is not the one, what of your other suspects?"

"Which suspects?" Roe asked rhetorically. "There are more

than two hundred of them, sir—including your own good self."

"I beg your pardon?"

"Every resident of Buck House who doesn't have an alibi for last Tuesday evening is a potential suspect. One or two have possible motives that we know about, but there could well be others with stronger motives that we haven't yet discovered. It's likely that the girl was a blackmailer: she tried it on with her former mistress and she had more money in her possession than can be easily explained away. You wouldn't happen to know, Sir Wilfred, if any of your gentlemen at court have a penchant for girls of the lower orders?"

"Good God, I hope not."

"It isn't all that unusual—especially among the aristocracy." Roe caught Gardner's eye and winked. Examination of the Threlfall and Watts dinner jackets had proved negative as expected and they had agreed that no purpose could now be served by discrediting their noble owner.

"And I suppose we still can't rule out the possibility of a homicidal maniac," Botterell put in.

"Which fortunately becomes less likely as time goes by without a repetition," said the A.C.

"A negative satisfaction," the Commissioner said. "Though once we succeed in nailing the fellow it might be best if he *is* mad enough to be put away without trial."

"That is something that certainly couldn't be kept quiet," Sir Wilfred observed. "So assuming the man is caught and found fit to stand trial the story is bound to come out eventually."

"For that very reason," the A.C. said, "I wonder whether all this secrecy must still be considered essential once the Jubilee is over. If we haven't got our man by then, it'll be chiefly due to the necessity of finding a murderer without revealing the fact there's been a murder. Take the brakes off my men and I've no doubt whatever they'll soon bring him in."

"I agree," said the Commissioner. "But that is a decision we don't have to take now. It would be disastrous for the news to break during the celebration period." Nobody queried that. "Anything else, gentlemen?"

Sir Wilfred Jennings said, "Yes, Commissioner. The matter of the inquest on Gill. I'm afraid I've been having difficulties with the two doctors involved."

"*Two* doctors?"

"Dr Abercrombie, the King's Coroner, and Dr Flint who certified the girl's death."

The Commissioner frowned. "I thought we decided we could keep Dr Abercrombie out of it. The girl was supposed to have died in the ambulance once it was beyond the Royal precincts, which would have made it no concern of the King's Coroner."

"I know, I know," Sir Wilfred nodded. "But Fergus Abercrombie heard about the accident and wanted to know the facts behind it: who attended Gill and whether it was certain she was still alive when she was carried out of the Palace. I had to put him in touch with Roger Flint and Flint was obliged to tell him the truth, said he'd be struck off the medical register if it came out he'd lied to a coroner—especially that particular one. Abercrombie came storming back to me, furious he hadn't been told in the first place. Since the girl actually died in the Palace he insists he'll have to preside over an inquest to be held in one of the Royal residences, according to the constitution. And he won't stand for any nonsense about an accident, it'll be a verdict of murder."

"So even without a trial it's bound to become public," the Commissioner said gloomily.

"No, sir, not necessarily. I discussed that at length with Abercrombie and I think I made him see how desirable it is for a public showdown to be avoided if we can possibly manage it. Nothing will shake him from the necessity of holding an inquest —perhaps at St James's Palace—but he agreed with some reluctance that it might be held *in camera*, with those already in the know as the only witnesses. It would not be entered in the official records and the Press of course would not be notified."

"What about the inquest they do have to be told about?" Gardner asked. "The one on the Buckingham Palace servant who died on her way to hospital after falling off a ladder. That'll still have to go ahead."

"We discussed that too," Sir Wilfred said. "It seems there is nothing in law against the holding of two separate inquests on the same body, though I doubt it's ever previously happened. The second one will be conducted by the Westminster Coroner, who will naturally have to be taken into our confidence, so that any questions he puts to Dr Flint will be framed to spare the doctor from committing perjury. All this subterfuge is of course quite deplorable, but in the circumstances—"

The telephone rang. The Commissioner answered it and passed it over to Roe, who spoke quietly while the discussion continued.

"Excuse me, gentlemen." Roe quelled the talk as he hung up. "That was my man at the Palace. The window cleaner Sam Riley turned up there this morning and clocked in for work."

21

"Why, Riley, why? What made you do it?"

To Harry Bennett, Clara's window cleaner was flattered by Veronica's description, obtained at second-hand from Daisy Brett before the subject had been living rough for three days. Confronted across Chief Inspector Botterell's desk by the stubbled, battered face, the coarse black untended hair, the rotting teeth and the stocky body, which he could smell from where he sat, Harry parted with any remaining shreds of pity for Alice Gill whose spite and lack of fastidiousness had induced her to offer herself to this creature.

"Why?" he repeated in the absence of an answer. "You must have had some reason for walking out of your digs, telling lies about burying your dead father, going into hiding and giving your work a miss."

An indulgent nod. "You're right, sir. I had me reason."

"Are you going to tell me?"

"Why, sir? Haven't I me own right to ask the question? Is it any law I have broken? A matter for the police, is it?"

"Anyone in royal employ who goes missing at a time like this becomes suspect, Riley."

"And meself coming from over the water?"

"That was partly the reason for our concern."

A carious grin. "You'll not be thinking I'm one o' them I.R.A.

bastards? Brought up Protestant, I was. No politics for me, sir—I spit on all their politics."

He looked as if he might give expression to his words and Harry said quickly, "Well, at least that's sensible. Why then do you have to act so suspiciously?"

A long pause. The workings of the untrained mind could almost be heard ticking over. "If I was to tell you, sir, would you be taking it any further?"

"Not if it's within the law, that I promise you."

"To be owing someone a pound or two, would the law be minding that?"

"This limb of the law certainly wouldn't. I am here, Riley, for security purposes only. If you ran off simply to avoid a debt, for God's sake come clean with me and I won't be troubling you any more."

Further hesitation. Then, "I'm thinking you seem a decent sort of feller. All right, sir, I'll trust you. It's this young girl, see. Lives near where I've been living in Kilburn. Some feller gives her a baby. There's a dozen or more she can pick from, but it has to be poor old Sam Riley she jumps on, seeing as I'm in regular work at a place like this. The bloody old beak sez I'm to pay for what I done—ten shillings a week. Ten shillings a bloody week for a poor man like me! Well, I do me best but I can't help getting a bit be'ind, can I now?—stands to reason. She threatens she'll take me to court again. Then on top of all me worry I'm told there's another girl I've been with has gone and got herself pregnant and sez it's me to blame."

"Wait a minute. What girl was this?"

"One of the girls here. Name of Alice. Same old story! I'd only been with the little bitch once, so why me? It was more'n I could take, sir. I reckoned I'd have to give up me job and start all over again somewhere else. Couldn't stand another ten bob a week, I couldn't."

"Who told you about Alice being pregnant?"

"The one she shared a room with—Clara Watson. We went out a few times, Clara and me, then she cuts up rough 'cause she finds out I'd been with Alice. Wouldn't have no more to do with me. Then last Tuesday I'm doing the winders in the Bow Room and I see Clara there with her feather duster. I had a few words with her, trying to make it up like, and that's when she tells me about Alice bein' in pup and sez it's going to cost me plenty and serve me bloody right."

Blast that wretched Clara! No mention of those malicious words in her version of the encounter.

"So you panicked. Decided to do a bunk."

A sheepish nod. "Seemed to me there wasn't nothing else for it. But I'm too worried to have me wits about me, buggerin' off like that without me insurance card. It comes to me later I'll be needing that card if I'm to get another job. Then I think I'll find me mate Pat Brennan as works here too and ask if he can nick it for me—I knew where Mr Gedge keeps them cards. I go last night to the Crown in Cricklewood where Pat does his drinking and there sure enough the man is. We has a jar together and he tells me that Alice Gill has fell off a ladder and broke her neck. Means there's not going to be a baby after all. I reckon I didn't ought to be glad about a thing like that, but it's been a big relief to me, I can tell you—I'm only 'uman. There's no reason any more for making meself scarce, so I come back here this morning and pick up me week's wages and tell Mr Gedge I'm wanting to carry on. And that's all God's own truth, sir."

Harry didn't seriously doubt it. Chief Inspector Botterell came in while he was winding up the interview. "You must understand, Riley, I have to check your story." He passed over pen and paper. "Write down the name and address of that girl with the affiliation order against you." And as the Irishman laboriously complied, "If you want my advice you'll stick to the beer in future. It comes cheaper."

"You're right, sir. I'll be keeping it buttoned up now, that's a promise."

He left them.

"No longer among our favourites, I gather," Botterell said.

"I'd say we can scratch him, sir." Harry gave a summary of what he had been told.

"You're probably right," Botterell agreed. "It's shaken them a bit at the Yard, losing one of our prime suspects. But I think we may have something rather valuable here." He took an envelope from his pocket. "Addressed to Frank Craddock and intercepted by the Palace postmaster. I've steamed it open. I'm beginning to understand now why he's been so cagey with you."

He extracted a single sheet of writing paper. No headed address, no date. The note said:

My love—Sunday n.g.—others here. Make it Monday morning. He will be upstairs watching procession. Green Room 9.30. *Don't* fail me, cut work if nec. This is *v. important.* I love you.

No signature.

"I'd say a girl's hand, fairly young one too," Botterell guessed.

Harry agreed. "Bit of a scrawl but what I'd call an educated scrawl. We'll get an expert on to it of course but I'll be surprised if he tells us different. Is there a Green Room here in the Palace?"

"There's the Green Drawing Room, but it doesn't sound to me like that one. It's on the first floor and looks out over the inner court. She'd hardly say 'He'—whoever he is—would be upstairs, she'd say he'd be out in front."

"So—a theatre?"

Botterell nodded. "That's more like it. They all have Green Rooms, don't they?"

"Let's see—which theatres are on the procession route . . .?"

"All those along the Strand. Adelphi, Vaudeville, Lyceum, Gaiety. Could be dating some actress or chorus girl, couldn't he?"

"I suppose so," Harry said. "But why then didn't he come out with it when I was questioning him? No need to protect her from me."

"If it's a clandestine affair he'd want to keep it dark in case 'He' should find out. So who's 'He'?—this bloke who's going to be watching the procession while Craddock has his oats down in the Green Room. Husband, father, boss?"

"It doesn't really matter, does it, sir? If that theory is the right one it has no bearing whatever on the killing of Alice Gill."

"Unless she kicked up awkward because he'd found himself a new girl friend."

"But she'd already found herself a new boy friend—and I don't mean that stinking window cleaner. Someone from outside the Palace called Leon or Leonard."

"Well, at least we can soon find out what Craddock is up to,"

Botterell said.

"That's right, sir. We keep this letter back from him till Monday—it's been delayed in the mail. Tomorrow he goes blundering all innocent to his cancelled date, poor chap, and we have somebody on his tail."

"Miss Knight?"

"Who else?" Harry said.

22

Much as she welcomed a temporary return to conventional police duty on Sunday afternoon, Veronica Knight was not happy about the nature of the task she was to fulfil. The order from Deputy Commander Roe to encourage an approach by the susceptible and strikingly handsome young footman was hardly one to strike dismay in a normally sexed girl of some experience, and Veronica had been ready enough to place herself at Frank Craddock's disposal. The result had left her not only frustrated and humiliated but, for one of the few times in her career, with a sense of having fallen down badly on her job. Hard as she had tried—and no shameless trollop could have tried harder—Frank Craddock showed not the least inclination to get to know her.

At meals in the servants' hall she would catch his eye as if by accident and smile across the tables, only to receive a blank stare. Ascertaining his various duties, she found jobs for herself that would bring her fortuitously into his presence. He brushed her off with a lofty recognition of her ardour that maddened her more than his indifference.

Others noticed and were also amused by her lovesick machinations. "Fair gone on our Frank, aren't you?" Daisy Brett remarked.

Veronica did her best to blush. "I think he's lovely!"

"And he hasn't given you a tumble?"

"Won't hardly look at me. Do you think it's because of that dead girl?—the one whose place I've taken."

"Shouldn't think so," Daisy said. "They broke up quite a

while back. Know what I reckon?—he's in love."

"Who with?"

"Nobody in Buck House, that I'm sure of—I don't miss much of the gossip that goes on here. And it's not just this last week he's been different. Must be a month or more since he packed up his old fun and games. You'd never have complained he wouldn't look at you then! There was none of us safe with the Frank we used to know. He even had a go at me once or twice and I'm no oil painting."

Veronica sighed. "Looks like I've missed the boat."

She had had a similar lack of success with her efforts to find out whether any suitors from inside the Palace—Sam Riley apart—had been favoured by Alice in succession to Craddock. She could sense a reluctance to talk about Alice, she was sure this was not for any reason demanding investigation but simply because death to the young was too unpopular a subject for idle conversation. It appeared generally accepted that Alice had lately had an outside interest—or interests. One being presumably her Leon or Leonard?

As to Clara Watson, neither Roe's appraisal nor Calkin's report could alter Veronica's growing conviction that her room companion was no murderess. To sleep so easily and so soundly, to enjoy in her phlegmatic way the repartee of the servants' hall, to answer Veronica's subtly loaded questions with utter detachment—all that after battering another girl to death? She'd have to be schizophrenic or otherwise insane, whereas in Veronica's opinion Clara was—blessedly for her, in view of her ghastly upbringing—nothing more than a dull, unimaginative bumpkin.

But a first-rate housemaid! Veronica envied her the uncomplaining ease with which she went about their tedious and exacting tasks. She herself was constantly in Ellen Carter's bad books, usually for being dilatory—some deliberate dawdling in order to meet up with Frank Craddock was partly responsible for that—but also because she had soon to acknowledge that 'Vera' was a congenital duffer at this kind of work.

Without Daisy's help on Friday morning her vain efforts to lay and light an 'economy fire' according to the head housemaid's specification almost drove her to ludicrous tears. She had seen Miss Carter patrolling this section of the Palace and was dismally prepared for further admonishment to which there could be no spirited response.

She feared the moment had come when someone quietly entered Lady Ruxford's sitting-room while she was still on her knees at the grate. It turned out that she was to receive help from an unexpected quarter. For the second morning in succession Lady Rosalie Carpender was paying an early call; she was again wearing the grey fur coat but now over a white sweater and navy skirt.

"Hullo—it's Vera, isn't it?" The girl spoke barely above a whisper. "Is Lucy about yet?—Lucy Grant, my mother's maid."

"I haven't seen her this morning, Miss."

"Damn . . . Do you know where her room is, Vera?"

"Afraid I don't."

"Pop out and ask somebody, will you? I'll take over your fire, it's not all that long since I was a Girl Guide . . . My God, what a cock-eyed way of building the damn thing."

Veronica said helplessly, "I know, it's how I've been told I've got to do it."

"Well, I'm going to start it again." She was on her knees now, dismantling the carefully piled up coals and clinkers. "Go on, Vera, buzz off and find out . . . No, don't bother, forget it."

The bedroom door had opened. Lady Rosalie rose to her feet as her mother came in, peignoir over nightdress. Lady Ruxford's eyebrows went up.

"Rosalie! Good heavens, child, not up all night again?"

"No, Mummy, I couldn't sleep."

"Makes two of us. It's probably this change in the weather." A wintry spring was at last showing promise of summer.

Lady Rosalie said, "I wasn't going to disturb you, I really came to see Lucy. I want to put my pearls in the safe at the house and you two are the only ones with the key."

"Why the worry all of a sudden? You haven't bothered till now."

"It's all these burglaries. They broke into the Glenisters' the night before last—Cicely had two lovely bracelets stolen."

"I thought you weren't on speaking terms with Cicely."

"Her brother Alan told me. Wasn't it lucky I'd already left? I might have lost my glorious pearls. And Penelope Frampton's mother had half her jewellery pinched on Wednesday night—"

The conversation came to an abrupt halt. Veronica, rebuilding her fire, guessed it had been terminated by a *pas devant les domestiques* look. Lady Ruxford addressed her.

"Leave that, girl. I shan't be needing a fire today. Go and get my tea."

Veronica stood up. "Very good, m'lady."

The sound of somebody vigorously stirring a spoon in a tumbler reached her as she approached the housemaids' pantry. Frank Craddock was mixing bicarbonate of soda for Mr Goodship, who had been awakened early by indigestion. Their meeting this time was coincidental, but Craddock was not to know that. He faced her with open exasperation.

"Oh, Christ—not again! Won't you ever let up?"

She blinked at him. "I don't know what you're talking about."

"Oh yes, you do. You're wasting your time, I'm not interested. Get that into your silly head. You're not my type."

Frank Craddock had been in a black mood since his summons to the Palace Steward's office, and the new housemaid's unashamed advances were an additional irritation to him. He was unsure whether his demotion had been the result of a complaint by the King about his usurpation of a page's duty or whether it might be due to an adverse report on him by the visiting Scotland Yard man. He was positive it was not for the reason given by Mr Goodship, that in fairness others should at this time be allowed to act in rotation as close waiter.

The descent from King's man to the lower rungs of the footmen's roster was steep and humiliating. His work now consisted of distributing mail and newspapers, raking up office fires, waiting on nonentities, and—worst of all—undertaking corridor duty. This involved carrying dishes for the best part of half a mile from the kitchens to the Royal Dining Room. Mounted on methylated spirit stoves under vast gleaming covers known as 'sluggers', they were still barely warm enough to please the royal palates by the time they reached the end of their journey and it was the carrier who was made the scapegoat for the idiocy of the system. Spills being inevitable, the footman on corridor duty had to discard his scarlet uniform for 'black Oxfords'—black tail-coat, black trousers, black leather Wellingtons: a contrast to his usual splendour and depressing in itself.

Unaware of what lay behind Frank's surliness, Veronica attributed it to some injudicious but well-meant words that Daisy had brightly said she had spoken to him on her friend's behalf.

"Which is why you'd be better advised to follow him yourself tomorrow," Veronica told Harry Bennett on Saturday morning. "Or couldn't it be one of your C.I.D. men? He wouldn't have to be told he was tailing a murder suspect."

"Craddock may not even be that," Harry said wearily. "But he's the nearest approach to it we're left with now. And your reasoning is all wrong, Speedy. You've just made it plain you're even better fitted for the job than I thought. If he happened to spot one of our men on his tail we might lose a valuable lead, whereas he won't worry so much if he sees you coming after him. He'll reach the obvious conclusion—no thought of the police— and tell you to take a running jump."

Harry added with not altogether mock severity, "And you'd best take that jump into the Thames if you bungle this one!"

23

Veronica slept fitfully that night. She had never tailed a suspect before and was tormented by the varied possibilities of failure. She would lose him among the sightseeing crowds converging on the centre of the capital on this Jubilee Eve, he would jump on a nearly full bus and it would be her luck if he were the last passenger allowed in, or if the only available seat were close by him. He might even hail a taxi, though on his wages that seemed unlikely—and she was sure it was only in the films that another was conveniently to hand for one to cry, "Follow that cab!"

Worst of all was the fear that her quarry might slip out of the Palace unseen by her, in spite of Harry Bennett having ascertained from Mr Goodship that Craddock would not be released from his duties till three o'clock. In the event, Veronica found she could have spared herself that last worry; but it was not without a troublesome interlude that she gained her own release.

"Afternoon off?" the head housemaid exclaimed in disbelief. "Certainly not. Why, you haven't been here a week yet. Every other Sunday I told you, starting with the second one."

"It's rather special, Miss Carter." The truthful part of the plea. "My mother is passing through London on her way to visit her sister up north. I do so want to meet her and tell her about my new job."

"I'm sorry, Knight, but rules are rules. It's quite impossible." Ellen Carter swung round and strode away to dispense with further argument.

Veronica was obliged to report the hitch to Mrs Wells, for which she was not thanked by the assistant housekeeper. "It's most unfortunate. The last thing I want is to upset my head housemaid."

"The last thing I want," Veronica retorted, "is to stay a housemaid at Buckingham Palace. If what I am doing today will bring this case any nearer to conclusion . . ."

Mrs Wells took over. "Let us sincerely hope it will. It has all been most unsettling."

"Especially for Alice Gill!"

"She at least knew how to do her work properly. The reports I have on yours are anything but satisfactory. Very well, Knight, it seems I have no choice, I shall have to tell Carter I've given you permission to go out this afternoon."

"Thank you, madam." An unnecessary reversion to her rôle of which Veronica later felt slightly ashamed.

She was changing to go out shortly after half past two when her bedroom door was crashed open by a livid Ellen Carter.

"You sneaky little bitch! How dare you go whining behind my back to Mrs Wells!"

Veronica said hotly, "You forced me to, I was sure she wouldn't be so spiteful. And I'll thank you not to call me dirty names."

"You'll get worse than names, my girl, if I have any more of your bloody sauce."

"Are you threatening me, Miss Carter?"

Raise a hand to me and you'll enter the betting as a suspect . . .

"I'm warning you I'm not the sort to make an enemy of—as more than one slut before you has found out."

She slammed out, promptly lengthening her odds with her last words, which she would surely have suppressed had Alice Gill been among her victims.

Inspector Calkin was waiting in plain clothes outside the staff entrance. A slight jerk of the head was his only recognition of Veronica's appearance. She moved in the indicated direction. A parking space in which tradesmen's vans were unloaded was empty on this Sunday afternoon but for a black Daimler saloon. Veronica walked to it, looked round, received a nod from Calkin and entered the back of the car through a door with a blue glass window. The car was one of the Royal Daimler fleet but lacked the usual shield with the Royal Arms on the front of its roof, being reserved for use by members of the Family wishing to travel unnoticed.

It had been parked with care. Sitting where possibly one of the Princes had preceded her, Veronica could obtain a clear view of the staff entrance without herself being seen. She glanced at her watch—2.52. Others of the staff, maybe jumping the gun, were beginning to emerge for their Sunday outing. At a break in the exodus just before three o'clock, Inspector Calkin strolled over and got in beside her.

"Shouldn't be long now. Nervous?"

"A bit." She realized she had been ruining the handle of her bag by continuous twisting.

"I wish I could tell you it's easier than you think, but up till this week I'd seldom been out of uniform." He took out a packet of cigarettes, then put it away again. "No, best not risk the smoke getting out. This car has to look unoccupied."

"I'll be all right, sir, once I get started."

He smiled. "Spoken like a true actress."

"But one who's miscast as a housemaid!"

She was treating him to a wry account of her recent tribulations when he gripped her arm. "Craddock . . ."

The tall footman was coming out alone, smartly dressed in a grey flannel suit with blue and white spotted tie and a dark brown flat-brimmed hat pulled down in front. He crossed the forecourt without glancing at the Daimler and turned left outside the gate. Veronica opened her door and jumped out, too tense to acknowledge Calkin's whispered "Good luck!"

Buckingham Gate was more crowded than she had anticipated

and in these first moments of the chase she was shaken by the fear
that he was already lost to her; then, thanks to his distinguishing
height, she spotted him stepping off the kerb to avoid a knot of
sightseers gazing through the railings at the parade ground on
the south side of the Palace. He was moving fast and she was
obliged to hurry at a pace that drew some curious glances,
thankful now for the mass of people continually checking his
long stride.

It seemed clear now that he intended walking to his destin-
ation, which came as some relief despite the strain of keeping up
with him. He passed the main gates of the Palace some fifteen
yards ahead of her and turned half left into Constitution Hill on
the outward route of tomorrow's procession, now an avenue of
white and scarlet banners stirred by a gentle spring breeze. Here
workmen were hammering and levering finishing touches to
temporary wooden stands. The crowds had thinned out and
Veronica was afraid that if Craddock were to turn his eyes would
be drawn to her scurrying figure before she had time to
slow.

Blessedly it never happened: he maintained his rapid progress
to Hyde Park Corner as though grudging a second's delay in the
keeping of his tryst. Knowing the disappointment awaiting him,
Veronica could not help feeling sorry for the eager young lover.

Turning left again into Grosvenor Place, Craddock paused at
the pavement's edge to await a break in the passing traffic.
Veronica slowed to a dawdle and watched him dart across the
road when only one as agile would have dared it. Marooned on
the other side, she had a moment of panic lest he made his way
down Grosvenor Crescent and shed her from his track before she
could make the crossing. Instead, to her relief, he turned left once
more and almost immediately was lost to view as he descended
the area steps of one of the massive Victorian houses near the top
of Grosvenor Place.

The traffic eased up. She crossed and walked past the area
railings with a wary downward glance. No sign: he'd been
admitted or let himself into No 96.

Another temporary stand had been erected opposite the gaily
decorated frontage of St George's Hospital. A few tired souls
were resting themselves on its lower tiers. Veronica recrossed

the road and joined them, seating herself where she could keep a watchful eye on No 96.

Ninety-six . . . Why was that number somehow familiar? But of course!

24

These days the London seat of the Earl and Countess of Ruxford could hardly be said to justify its existence as a private house. Not even the Silver Jubilee could drag the war-scarred earl to London, and his wife's visits were confined largely to her periodical fortnight duties as a Lady of the Bedchamber, when it was necessary for her to reside at Buckingham Palace.

Most of the neighbouring houses in Grosvenor Place had now 'gone commercial' and Lord Ruxford had received several approaches from property dealers anxious to convert No 96 into office premises. He had given none of them serious consideration. The house had been in his family for three generations; he was a conservationist with sentimental memories of childhood days spent there; and he had no pressing need of the handsome return that a sale would undoubtedly bring. Besides, his daughter Rosalie, now approaching eighteen, would be 'coming out' next year, when the house would be reopened for the season and echo again to the music and laughter of youth.

Meanwhile, its rooms were shrouded in dust-sheets and its only permanent occupants were its caretakers, the Hendersons, an elderly couple who had long been in the Ruxford service; he was a former butler, she had been Lucy Grant's predecessor as Lady Ruxford's personal maid.

Her ladyship was a frequent visitor to the house during her spells of attendance at the Palace, for it was here that she kept the clothes she required mainly for town wear; she also used the safe in the study for some of her jewellery, though the more valuable pieces were normally kept in a bank's safe deposit.

Tomorrow Lady Ruxford was to ride in one of the state carriages behind Their Majesties with a maharajah as her companion. On this Sunday afternoon she and Lucy were engaged in the important task of deciding on the most suitable gown, hat and fur cape for the occasion.

The choice was eventually made from the many articles of wear spread about the second-floor boudoir and bedroom, and Lucy inquired, "And the pearl necklace, m'lady?"

"Yes, I think so. And that reminds me, I have Rosalie's pearls here, she wants them put in the safe. I'll go down to the study while you pack up."

As she reached the first-floor landing a sound from below checked Lady Ruxford's descent. Somebody was coming up the stairs from the kitchen quarters. It could hardly be one of the Hendersons, who had left together nearly an hour ago on their usual Sunday visit to relatives; and Rosalie would naturally have entered the house by the front door.

Lady Ruxford stepped cautiously to the balustrade and stared down into the hall. A squeak as the baize door from the back stairs was pushed open, then she had a momentary glimpse of a figure crossing the hall, a man in a grey suit and brown felt hat, his face indiscernible from the floor above. She expected him to be making for the study, where the safe was to be found, but instead he passed its door and went into the Green Room beyond.

This was a little-used room facing on to the yard and small garden at the back of the house. Originally it had been called the Music Room, but since nobody in the present family could play its grand piano—or indeed any other musical instrument—it had in recent years become more aptly known by its decor.

What could there be in that room to attract a burglar before anything else? Why had he by-passed both study and dining-room? Could he perhaps be planning a systematic search of the house believing it to be safely empty? These thoughts raced through Lady Ruxford's mind as she ran breathlessly back up the stairs to her bedroom.

"Lucy—a burglar! He's downstairs in the Green Room." She hurried to the telephone.

"The Green Room, m'lady?" Her maid echoed her surprise as she moved towards the door.

Lady Ruxford said, "Lucy, come back! Where are you going?"

"The key ought to be on the outside, I'll lock him in there."

"No—stop! He may come out and attack you . . . "

But Lucy Grant was a policeman's daughter. As her mistress dialled the emergency service, she kicked off her shoes and ran silently down the two flights of stairs.

The door of the Green Room had been left a few inches open. She heard a movement inside as she tiptoed to it but was unable to see the intruder round it. The key, as anticipated, was still in the door on the outside. Taking a deep breath, Lucy grasped the handle, slammed the door, turned the key.

On its other side Frank Craddock froze. He had barely recovered from the surprise and disappointment of finding the Green Room empty. So different an arrival from last time . . . Then, as today, he had let himself in with the basement key given him by his darling, only then she had been awaiting him here on the unshrouded sofa, arms held out to clasp him to her, blue eyes joyously sparkling and those tremulous lips parted in eager summons. Now . . . Christ, he was trapped! Somebody else was here and had seen him, somebody making nonsense of her confidence that they'd be alone. Why in God's name hadn't she stayed outside to warn him off?

He only became aware that there was a telephone in the room when a tinkling note told of a receiver being replaced elsewhere in the house. Obvious now that the police would soon be here. Craddock ran to the window, forced up the old-fashioned sash. A drop of some fifteen feet to the yard, but fortunately Victorian plumbing had provided an outside wastepipe curving down within grasping distance from an upstairs bathroom.

He started to climb out of the window, then checked himself at the realization that they'd anticipate this move and be watching out for his appearance. Lady Ruxford or Lucy Grant—the two most likely to be here in the house—could hardly fail to recognize their ex-footman. Better they should take him for a common thief . . .

From his breast pocket he whipped out the blue and white spotted handkerchief matching his tie. Wrenching off the tie, he hastily covered the lower part of his face with a makeshift mask. He clambered through the window, raised himself to a standing position on the outer sill, grabbed the curving wastepipe and swung his legs free. Half a century of exposure to London's weather had rendered the pipe incapable of taking his weight: it parted from the wall, bent outward as he dangled from it, then slowly bowed over and dropped him with merciful gentleness into the yard.

Jarred but unhurt he scrambled up and made a dash for the green gate in the brick wall bounding the garden, praying he would find it unlocked. It was. A woman's shrill voice cried "Stop thief!" from above as he flung himself through it, tearing off and pocketing his rudimentary mask on its other side.

The narrow back street was luckily bare of witnesses except for a woman wheeling a pram who came to a stop and gaped in silent alarm as he turned his back on her and darted into Grosvenor Crescent, where he slowed to as fast a walk as he dared, heading for the crowded safety of Hyde Park Corner.

Intent on removing himself from the scene as rapidly and as far as possible, he was only stayed from another dash through the traffic by the bell of an approaching police car. The car with three men in it swung round from Piccadilly and slewed across the northbound traffic in Grosvenor Place, squealing to a stop outside No. 96. Craddock took advantage of the temporary hold-up it had brought about, crossing with the vague intention of escaping in the direction whence it had come, knowing that by now they'd be giving his description—"Grey suit, brown hat, can't have got far"—and reasoning that the police might first discount the possibility that he was heading for their own station.

As he hurried past the people resting near the foot of the newly erected stand a voice called, "Frank!" He pulled up and turned as if lassooed, then moved without hesitation to where she sat smiling.

"Don't tell me you're still following me around!"

"Quite by chance, Mr Conceited."

"This time you couldn't be more welcome. Stand up, please. Come for a walk." And as she obliged with what she hoped was a wondering look, "Mind if I put an arm round you?"

"My, what a change!"

Had he but known it Veronica was as eager to grant him protection as he was to receive it. There could be no question of her revealing her true identity in his presence were he to be apprehended; she'd have to insist on being taken to the station with him even if it meant assaulting a police officer. Once there she could safely make herself known and get him cleared, if necessary putting them on to Roe at the Yard; but she wouldn't be thanked for it by Roe or anyone else, since it would inevitably lead to dangerous speculation on why a policewoman attached to C.I.D. should be keeping surveillance on a Buckingham Palace footman.

Veronica had by now deduced a fairly clear picture of what had been going on. Lady Rosalie Carpender!—"proper little tart" according to Alice Gill as reported by Daisy Brett. Small wonder Frank had been at pains to hide the affair from Harry Bennett. To use the Ruxford house as a rendezvous was surely the true reason for young Rosalie's eagerness to move in there. By intercepting her note cancelling today's assignation they had nearly exposed the ill-assorted lovers to the girl's mother. Nearly but presumably not quite, because the police would surely not have been summoned had Frank Craddock been recognized.

"We'll walk in the park," he was saying. "Sorry I was rude to you the other morning. I didn't mean it, I think you're super."

She could feel him trembling and said so. "You don't have to be nervous with me, Frank."

He said hoarsely, "It's not what you think, Vera. Look, if a copper comes along, starts asking questions, you've been with me for the last hour or so. O.K.?"

She blinked round at him. "What *have* you been up to, Frank?" Pity they didn't give Oscars for C.I.D. performances . . .

"I had a date with my girl," he said. "She's a maid at one of the big houses down there. She said the people were away and we'd be alone this afternoon, but she was wrong—the lady of the house had come back. Thought I was a burglar, I reckon, and rang for the police. Saw 'em arriving just now, did you? They're after me."

"Oh, you poor man. I don't wonder you're shaking."

"You'll do what I ask?"

She nodded, "Course I will. We came out of the Palace together, walked all the way here, never been parted one minute. It's not as if you was dressed much different from lots of other men. Look, there's a bloke over there with another grey suit and your sort of hat."

"Let's hope it's him they pounce on!" He squeezed her gratefully. "I love you, Vera."

"No, you don't," Veronica said. "You're in love with her,
aren't you?"

He said diffidently, "Yes. Very much, I'm afraid."

"Nothing to be afraid of, I understand. What's her name?"

"Her name? It's—Rose."

"You must think I'm a fast one," she said. "Flirting with you
like I did—oh, I admit it. You see, they told me you hadn't got a
girl. She died, they said, and I'd been taken on in her place. You
was looking so sad the first time I saw you I thought I'd try and
take her place with you as well, see if I could help you to forget
her. And all the time you was in love with someone else!"

"That's right," he said. "I've stopped even looking at other
girls now I've got Rose."

"Is she the reason you dropped the other one?"

"Alice? There was never much really between me and Alice. I
took her out a few times, she was pretty enough and—and
willing too. But I never did like her, she could be a proper bitch."

"What a thing to say about someone who's dead!"

"Her being dead doesn't alter facts."

"I wouldn't like to think of anyone talking like that about me
when I'm gone. What did she do to make you so bitter?"

He shrugged. "She was a bitch. That's enough about her. Tell
me about yourself, Vera . . . Oh, Christ, here we go!" A police
car had moved silently up behind them as they turned into the
park; it slowed and they were conscious of two pairs of eyes
sizing them up.

"Take no notice," Veronica said. "I've made a funny remark.
Laugh!" He responded well to her lead and the car moved on
again, eyes abandoning the cheerful young couple for another
potential quarry.

"My God, you're a cool one," Craddock said admiringly. "Tell
us the truth now: was it really just by chance you were there to
save me?"

She said with a nod, "I reckon it was fate. I came out for a bit of
a stroll, hadn't had a breath of fresh air since Wednesday. What's
the time, Frank?"

"Just on a quarter to four."

"I'll have to be getting back."

"Must you? I thought we might go and have a cup of tea at Lyons's."

"Another day," she said. "I left Daisy alone on our call, promised her I'd be back by half-four."

She considered it unlikely that she would get more of any value from Frank Craddock and doubted her ability to sustain a performance in which one slip could be disastrous.

"Think I'll go to the pictures," he said.

"Good idea. Stop there in the dark as long as possible, that's where you'll be safest. I'll stay with you as far as the Regal."

He shuddered. "Not that one, it's Shirley Temple."

"All right, the Marble Arch Pavilion."

There was an echoing groan from Harry Bennett when Veronica reported this exchange on her arrival back at the Palace. "I told Craddock I'd been to the Regal myself last week. He'll guess now I'm as big a liar as he is. Not that I blame him for playing the gallant gentleman. The young heiress and the under-footman! Shades of Lady Chatterley."

"Except she was a mature woman and this one's a silly little chit of seventeen."

He nodded. "There'd certainly be a flutter in the pigeon loft if that were to come out."

"Have you still got that note she sent him?" Veronica asked.

Harry produced it. "He'll be receiving it tomorrow morning. I think I know what you have in mind. Who's that 'He' who's going to be safely upstairs watching the procession?"

She nodded. "I have a theory." And as she studied the note. "Yes—I thought I remembered. She's blotted the 'e' of 'He'—or rather what we thought was 'He'. But looking at it again I think it's an 's'. The caretakers at Number Ninety-six are called Henderson: Lady Ruxford mentioned them while I was in there trying to get that damned fire lit. It's the 'Hs'—the Hendersons —who'll be upstairs and out of the way."

"Agreed! Good for you, Speedy." But he added on a dubious note, "Let's hope he'll still follow instructions after the scare he's had today."

"I'm betting he will. The way he talked of his 'Rose' I think he really is in love with that little floosie. And I'd bet twice as much he's far too soft to commit murder, even if he had a real motive. This squalid entanglement of theirs isn't going to help us much to get our hands on Alice's killer."

"You're probably right there," Harry conceded glumly. "But I'm taking nothing for granted. If their meeting tomorrow can provide one single clue . . . "

"Assuming it still takes place."

"Quite. But we've got to reckon it will." He sighed resignedly. "And if it does there'll be three of us who won't be seeing the King ride by."

25

"King's weather" they called it, and once again it had lived up to expectations, borrowing a day from high summer to bless the Silver Jubilee of King George V and Queen Mary. The sun had risen to shine from a cloudless sky, promising a busy time for the St John Ambulance Brigade and planning havoc among the ranks of the Royal Marines lining the route from the Palace in suffocatingly tight tunics.

The crowds bursting central London at its seams were patently going to justify the inevitable record claimed for them in next day's papers. It had been evident since dawn that a late riser could expect to catch no more than a fleeting glimpse of His Majesty's white plumes. Those in the forefront of the thronged pavements had been there all night; behind them packed stands had been closed long before the normal breakfast hour of most seat-holders. Summer dresses on their first outing sprinkled indiscriminate colour, laid on thickly here and there by detachments of Chelsea Pensioners, the Boys' Brigade, Sea Cadets, the Legion of Frontiersmen and children from the Foundling Hospital. Tree branches were tested by climbers daring enough to defy the police from on high, and the worthies of every convenient statue were joined by enthusiasts who reckoned the discomfort of their perches well worth enduring.

Their eventual reward was not to be shared by the one who huddled with similar lack of comfort and dignity beneath a sheet-covered grand piano at No. 96 Grosvenor Place. Detective Sergeant Bennett had taken up his vigil here shortly after 8.30 a.m. Gaining entry without upsetting the plans of the secret lovers had been a tricky business. Harry was accompanied to the house by Inspector Calkin in uniform. Unsure whether or not Lady Rosalie might be about, they took themselves to the basement door at the foot of the area steps. Old Henderson, who answered their knock, was a solemn-faced man of 70; he regarded them with the defensive appraisal that came naturally to an ex-butler opening a door to strangers.

The inspector introduced himself and his sergeant, both showing their warrant cards. "May we come in?" And as they were grudgingly admitted, "You, I believe, are Mr Henderson. Who else is in the house?"

"There's only me and the wife."

Harry said, "I understood Lady Rosalie Carpender has been staying here these last few nights."

"She's not here now. After the bit of trouble they had here yesterday her ladyship didn't want her stopping on. She's gone to stay with friends."

The two policemen heard this with mixed feelings. They were spared the feared possibility that the girl might become aware of their arrival, but were left uncertain whether she would now come back to keep the appointment she had initiated.

"It's because of what happened yesterday that we're here," Calkin said. "You were out, I believe, when Lady Ruxford disturbed the intruder."

Defensively, "Her ladyship knows we take Sunday afternoons off."

"So, it would seem, did the man who broke in."

"Have you caught him?" Mr Henderson had been joined by his wife, some ten years younger but of equally solemn expression.

"Won't be long now," Harry assured her. "He left some useful fingerprints, and knowing this man it's our guess he'll come back."

"Which is why I am leaving the sergeant with you," Calkin

said. "He'll explain what is required. I have to get back now to
my other duties. Please do exactly what Detective Sergeant
Bennett asks."

Henderson looked dubious. "We ought to have her ladyship's
authority."

"You can hardly reach her now, she'll be with the Queen,
getting ready for the procession. If you have any misgivings, Mr
Henderson, I suggest you ring Scotland Yard and speak to the
officer in charge of this case—Deputy Commander William
Roe."

Mrs Henderson said, "I wouldn't think it's necessary, John.
I'm glad we'll have a policeman here to protect us."

Upon which a relieved Inspector Calkin took his leave.

"The man we're after," Harry told the couple, "is a member of
a gang who have been responsible for a number of robberies
lately in high society. We've had a tip-off that they'll be oper-
ating again today while the procession is on. It's an ideal time for
a break-in, with a distraction like that keeping people on the
route up at their windows. You will be watching—where?"

"From the first floor balcony," Mrs Henderson said. "We have
chairs out there."

"Just the two of you?"

"That's all. Her ladyship did say I could ask my sister and her
husband, but they're both getting on, they decided they couldn't
face the crowds."

"Well, all I want from you is to show me the room where that
man was locked in yesterday."

"The Green Room," Mr Henderson prompted.

"Then back you go to your balcony and stay out there till the
procession has passed. I shall come and tell you when it's safe for
you to come down."

Harry's first sight of the Green Room brought a measure of
relief. The dust-sheets covering the furniture provided better
hiding facilities than he had experienced in some past eaves-
dropping ventures. He took note of the sofa on which the re-
union, were it to come, would presumably be staged, and the
welcome shape of a grand piano in the farther corner to the right
of the window from which Frank Craddock had made his escape.

He thanked the Hendersons and impressed final instructions

on them. "Now remember, this is a trap we're springing, so don't let anything you hear bring you back in from that balcony. Give the chap a scare and you might wreck this whole operation. I've got men posted outside who'll come in at my signal, so we're well equipped to deal with chummy—if, as I hope, he shows up." (My God, I'm almost beginning to believe it myself . . .)

He was satisfied that they would stay upstairs in ignorance of what might happen below. The lovers would in any case be at pains not to disturb them when making their separate entrances.

Left alone, Harry raised the covering from the piano and endorsed his immediate choice of it for his unsavoury purpose, for it would mercifully allow him a sitting position with sufficient of the wall covered on its far side to provide a back-rest. He rearranged the dust-sheet to ensure against any tell-tale gap and ducked under it to settle himself for his vigil.

Without the necessity as yet to suspend all movement he found himself in danger of being too much at ease. He had enjoyed considerably less than his normal ration of sleep during the four nights that had passed since he had been put on this most exacting of cases. With the streets around the house closed to traffic and the crowds still awaiting something to cheer, the strange London silence was soporific. He was shocked to realize that he had closed his eyes and begun to nod when a strident male voice jerked him into sudden alertness. It took him a moment to place it, then he remembered that broadcasting was to begin today an hour or so earlier than its usual 10.15 start. Loudspeakers had been installed along the processional route to relay the service from St Paul's Cathedral; there was evidently one above the stand at Hyde Park Corner.

Unnerved by his lapse, Harry welcomed the music that followed—loud enough to keep him awake but not too loud to drown the hoped-for exchange of confidences. Twenty-one minutes to go, if they were to be punctual and if—a double if—both were to keep the tryst. Until his meeting with the Hendersons this morning he had been convinced from the urgency of her note that Lady Rosalie would be here without fail. He was less sure about Craddock, especially after yesterday's events. Mr Brian Goodship, with whom he'd had a word, had undertaken to release several of the Palace footmen from their duties by 9 a.m.

on this special day—Frank Craddock notably among them.
Allow him time for a hurried change out of uniform, and if he
had the sense to stick to the back streets he'd have no need to keep
her waiting long . . . Assuming now that she could get away
from her friends and make it herself.

Nine fifteen. Loudspeaker rasping out military band's selec-
tion from *Showboat*.

Nine twenty. Ragged cheer from Hyde Park Corner as commentator described the scene at Hyde Park Corner.

Nine twenty-five. Treacle pouring through corrugated iron
roof—the inevitable cinema organ with *Smilin' Through*.

Nine thirty. Commentator on scene in forecourt of Buckingham Palace. Too loud and shrill, this one: don't get so excited,
man.

Nine thirty-two. Shut up out there! Thought I heard something . . . Was it? . . . No . . . Yes! Someone opening the
Green Room door.

Light footsteps, rapid feminine breathing as though she'd had
to make a run for it. She was crossing the room to the window.
Shapely ankles came within his view as she stood looking out at
the small back garden, near enough for him to have leant forward
and touched her.

The loudspeaker had gone dumb, bringing a temporary fright-
ening silence to the room. Come on, damn you—say something,
play something. Dust, keep out of my nostrils. Stomach—please,
please no gurgle . . .

Two, perhaps three minutes passed like hours, allowing her
panting to subside enough for him to catch the sudden gasp of
relief, followed at once by the disappearance of the ankles. At
least it would seem they were both here now, poor consolation
though it would be if their meeting were to prove this whole
mission a waste of time and nervous tension.

She was at the door to receive him. "Oh, darling—thank God! I
was afraid you wouldn't make it—I nearly didn't."

Pause for embrace; then from Craddock, "But didn't you sleep
here last night?"

"My mother wouldn't let me. Some man broke in here yesterday and—"

"That was me."

"What!"

"Your letter didn't arrive till this morning. I came in here expecting to find you same as usual and somebody locked me in."

"That was Lucy. My poor love!" Momentary draught as a dust-sheet was flung aside. Sound of sofa springs under pressure. "Mummy said it was a man in a mask and he jumped out of the window."

"That was me right enough. But they didn't know it was me, which is all that matters, isn't it, my darling?"

"Oh, Frank, you're wonderful!"

Lengthier pause for confirmation of her opinion.

Rosalie again: "Darling, I've wanted so desperately to see you since I heard about Alice."

"That was a bit of all right, wasn't it?"

"Was it?"

"What do you mean, sweetie? Best bit of luck we could have wished for."

"That's what I thought as soon as I heard. When that new maid told me she was dead I wanted to sing out loud at the top of my voice. Then when I started thinking about it—it seemed almost too good. Frank, tell me the truth. I won't stop loving you, darling, I swear it—I'll love you all the more, knowing you did it for me."

"Did what? I don't know what you're talking about."

"You did do it, didn't you? You killed Alice."

"*Killed* her? Christ—what sort of talk is this? Of course I didn't kill her! Nobody did. She fell off a ladder, it was an accident."

"Oh, my love, is that really true? Don't lie to me—please don't lie to me. You swear it was nothing to do with you?"

"I was never anywhere near the bloody girl. It was an accident I tell you."

"My mother doesn't think so. She thinks Alice was murdered."

"Go on!"

"I heard her talking to Lucy about it, she didn't know I was listening. She said there was a detective from Scotland Yard going around questioning all sorts of people at the Palace."

"You're telling me! He gave me a fair grilling. Wanted to know where I was that time I was with you. I said I'd gone to the pictures and picked up some girl there, but I don't think he believed me. I'd have been in all the more of a sweat if I'd thought he was on about a murder."

"That's only Mummy's idea, she may be wrong. But I can't tell you, my darling, what a relief this all is—I've been thinking such awful things. You do absolutely swear you had nothing to do with it?"

"Me—a murderer! I don't know how you could think such things."

"I wouldn't have blamed you—that horrid little blackmailing bitch. Murdered or not, she deserved all she got."

"Could be your mother was right," he said. "She put the black on us, so why not other people too? There's a few I could mention —some of the real nobs—that'd pay a lot to keep quiet what I know. They seem to think footmen don't have eyes or ears. If one of them's bumped her off, good luck to him I say."

"May he get away with it! Oh Frank, I'm so happy now. If you knew what I've been going through . . . "

"Sweetie, sweetie . . . "

Sounds of passion. His voice, hoarser now—"Sure it's O.K.?"

"They're out on the balcony, they won't come in till it's over. Love me, darling—love me, love me . . . Oh, that's gorgeous . . . "

Harry Bennett could recall no experience as embarrassing as this. Not only embarrassing but a disturbing challenge to his manhood. They were noisy in their ecstasies, too noisy for his attempted concentration on a description of the Prime Minister's procession now leaving Clarence Gate.

And as the six carriages proceed up the Mall with an escort of Metropolitan Mounted Police, back to the scene at Buckingham Palace . . .

The door of the Green Room crashed open.

"My God!" A woman's outraged voice.

Confusion of gasping and scuffling, then the girl's voice in tearful anger. "Get out, Lucy!"

"Don't you give *me* orders, you wicked girl. It's you that's getting out of here. Stop snivelling and try to make yourself decent, you look like the dirty little slut you are."

From Craddock, indignantly: "Don't you dare talk to her that way!"

"You shut your mouth, you filthy swine. I'll deal with you in a minute. I wouldn't have believed it, not again after that promise you gave me, that solemn promise. Out you go, my girl. Upstairs if you like, you can make some excuse to the Hendersons. Had a rough time getting here through the crowd from the looks of you. Go on, now—do what I say or I'll make you regret it. I want to talk to Frank."

Departing footsteps. Door slammed shut.

"That was a terrible thing to do, Miss Grant."

"So you said that other time—those very words. Expect me to apologize, do you? I warned you then, Frank, and I warned you again just the other day, when you both gave me your word you'd finish it. Now I know your promises are worth nothing I'll have to make sure you really do finish it this time."

"You had no right to make us promise a thing like that. We love each other."

Scornfully, "Love! You've only got one idea of love, Frank Craddock, and that's what you were at when I came in."

"It's not true. I love her and she loves me. Anyway, she's old enough now, you can't hold that against me."

"I can still report what I saw that day in Bredenham, they can still get you for that."

"But you won't, Miss Grant, I know that, because you couldn't do it without bringing her name into it."

"Oh, so you've got enough sense to see that. You're getting quite bright, Frank, and that's a big change. All right, so I'm not going to report you, but I'm going to see to it you never set eyes on that silly wicked young girl again."

"Oh, yes? I'd like to know how."

"I'm sending you on a nice long journey, my lad, that's how. Australia, New Zealand, Canada—I don't care which one it is, so long as there's a few thousand miles between you and Lady Rosalie."

"That's very interesting. And how am I supposed to get there —charter the Royal Yacht?" Chink of coins. "Right now, all I have in the world is twelve shillings and fourpence. That wouldn't get me as far as the Isle of Wight."

Rustling of paper. "You can go as far as you like with what I've got here. The farther the better."

"What's that?"

"Ninety-two pounds. It's what I got out for Alice, but it can be put to better use now. She asked for a hundred, it was the most I could manage."

Sudden change of tone. "All your savings? You're being very generous, Miss Grant, but I couldn't take that. I couldn't take it even if I had any intention of going."

"You're going, Frank—I'm making sure of that."

"You can't make me!"

"Can't I? Then we'll see what happens when I tell them you killed Alice Gill."

"You're daft. You've been listening to her ladyship, haven't you? Just because she's got some crack-brained idea—"

"Her ladyship is perfectly right, Frank. Not that she knows it, she was only guessing. But the police know it and I know it. Alice Gill was murdered."

In the Green Room a long moment of silence.

The Captain's Escort of the Royal Horse Guards stand motionless in the forecourt awaiting the bugle call that will signal the departure of the first carriage with the Duke and Duchess of York and the two little Princesses, looking very sweet in pink frocks and pink hats.

"How do you know that, Miss Grant?"

"Never you mind, I know. And I'll tell the police what I heard and saw last Tuesday night. How I opened the door of my lady's sitting-room and saw you creeping out of the Old Library. How you looked so furtive and frightened I waited till you'd gone, then I went along to the library to see what you'd been up to—and there was Alice lying on the floor with her head bashed in. I was so shaken and so scared I couldn't bring myself to tell anyone what I'd seen, specially as it meant I'd be sending you to the gallows. But now I can't keep it to myself any longer, I've got to come out with it."

"It's lies, it's all wicked lies! I had nothing at all to do with it, I haven't been anywhere near the Old Library, not for a month or more."

"But which one of us are they going to believe?"

"You couldn't do a thing like that to me!"

"Oh yes, I could—and what's more I will, you get that straight, unless you do what I'm telling you to. Take this money and get out. Pack up your things at the Palace, give in your notice and be off. And don't you dare try and get in touch with Lady Rosalie again or I go straight to the police with that story of mine."

"They'll think I'm guilty, disappearing like that."

"Doesn't matter what they think, without me they've got no proof. Now take this money and go."

"Tell me the truth, Miss Grant . . . "

"Take it I said!"

A flimsy white note dropped to the floor and came to rest an inch inside the dust-sheet hanging from the grand piano. Harry Bennett shrank back instinctively as Lucy Grant's hand reached down and picked it up.

"This one too—go on now. The streets are clear at the back, you can go out that way. And don't let me ever set eyes on you again."

"My Christ, but you're a dreadful woman!"

Now all is activity as the Sovereign's Escort form up to await the bugle call that will set the Royal Procession on its way. The Ninth Royal Lancers in their scarlet uniform, the Fifth Inniskilling Dragoon Guards in blue and green, the Life Guards in black and silver and scarlet . . .

The Green Room door closed. The covering was raised from the piano.

"You can come out from under there," she said calmly.

Harry wished ruefully that his situation allowed a more dignified emergence.

"How long have you known I was here?"

"I caught sight of a shoe when I stooped down to pick up that five-pound note."

"By which time it was too late!"

"Too late for what? To save myself?" She shook her head. "There was never any question of that. I was only waiting till today was over."

Harry said stiffly, "Lucy Grant, you are under arrest and I must warn you that anything you say will be taken down—"

"And used in evidence at my trial?" A sad little sceptical smile. "I don't think so. Not that I mind telling you, it hasn't been easy keeping it all to myself." She added quickly. "That doesn't mean I regret doing what I had to. It was the only way to deal with that poisonous creature."

Harry was satisfied to listen without comment.

"It actually started long before we knew there was a vile thing called Alice Gill in this world. Two years ago in fact, when Lady Rosalie was only fifteen." She paused in slight embarrassment.

"You surprised them as you did today?"

"Just the same. She was always a wilful, over-sexed girl and he's only got one idea in his head. What he was doing was criminal of course, but I'd say he was less than half to blame, he's a very handsome young man and I'm sure she led him on. How can it happen with fine and decent parents like she has? We were all at Bredenham then, his lordship's place in Suffolk. Frank Craddock was a footman there, I had just been appointed her ladyship's personal maid. If I hadn't dropped my duster out of that window it might all have blown up then . . . I was shaking out this duster, you see, and a gust of wind took it out of my fingers. It dropped on to the glass roof of the conservatory. I couldn't leave it there, it was too unsightly. I tried to think what I could get long enough to reach it with, and I thought I might do it with one of the cues from the billiards room. It was a room that was seldom used any longer, only when we had guests and that was rare—his lordship had become very withdrawn since he got back from the war.

"I went in to fetch a cue and there they were, on the long padded seat in there: Lady Rosalie, that young titled schoolgirl and one of our footmen! I was so shocked and stunned I thought I was going to faint. And I got out of the wretched child it wasn't the first time either. What was I to do? It couldn't be allowed to go on, that was plain, and I just couldn't bring myself to tell my lady what I'd seen, I think she'd have gone out of her mind.

"Then I thought of something. My young sister had just started work at the Hall and I could see she was a little bit gone on Frank, like so many of the young girls were. I didn't have any real fears for Jean, she was a decent sensible kid, but that wasn't what I told her ladyship. I said I was worried to death she'd let Frank Craddock seduce her. My lady was very sympathetic and of course she didn't want anything like that to happen between servants under her roof. She said she'd do her best to find Frank another place. That turned out to be Buckingham Palace because luckily he was the right height. So off he goes to London, then Lady Rosalie is sent to a finishing school in Paris, and I thought to myself that's done with, thank God, and he hasn't given her a baby, thank God twice over, and I don't have to worry about them any more. But I was wrong."

And now comes the great moment when the Royal Carriage sweeps out of the Palace grounds, drawn by six Windsor Greys with outriders from the Royal Mews in their tunics of gold with black velvet jockey caps . . .

"Very wrong," Miss Grant repeated. "She came back from France earlier this year and when she visited her mother at Buckingham Palace she went out of her way to find Frank and it started all over again. Or rather it hadn't really stopped because the stupid girl had been writing him letters all the time she was away—dreadful letters, dirty letters, you couldn't believe they'd been written by a decently brought up girl from one of the best families in the land. Once she was home the two of them started meeting in secret again, more than once in this very house when the caretakers were out.

"Till she came back Frank had been going with that little slut of a housemaid, and she didn't take kindly to being brushed off. She took to following him on his times off and she soon discovered who the new attraction was. Not only that but she somehow got hold of those letters, and to make things worse Frank couldn't remember how many of them he'd kept, so when she started her blackmail there was no knowing what she was still holding back.

"At first she wanted fifty pounds or she'd tell Lady Ruxford what was going on and give her one of those letters to prove it. Frank of course hadn't got any money, and it may surprise you but Rosalie didn't have that much either. I suppose like most people Alice thought a daughter of rich parents must be rich enough herself, but Rosalie doesn't come into any wealth of her own till she's eighteen, and her parents have never believed in giving her more pocket money than most girls of her age and class get. She had to pawn a diamond brooch to pay Alice off and get those letters back, and then she didn't get all of them.

"About a month later Alice said she had some more and this time it was going to cost a hundred pounds to buy them back, because she'd decided she could get that much by selling them to a gossip writer on one of the Sunday papers. In the meantime her ladyship had noticed that Rosalie wasn't wearing her brooch any more, and when she asked her about it Rosalie said she had lost it, so my lady said they must claim the insurance on it. That scared Rosalie, because it was a sort of criminal thing to do, and she didn't dare get rid of any other jewellery, not that she has a great deal. It was then she told me about it. I'd said once or twice I'd got a little nest-egg put by, and she asked me if I'd lend it her till her eighteenth birthday, and that's how it all came out.

"I've never come into contact before with a thing like blackmail, but I've heard often enough that no blackmailer is ever satisfied, they'll bleed you dry and then likely as not do what they've threatened all along. Aren't I right?"

Harry nodded.

"So even if we did get back all the letters there was nothing to stop Alice still telling her ladyship about it once she knew she wasn't being paid any more. And that was something I wasn't going to let happen, not if I had the strength to stop it. I've been in the service of Lord and Lady Ruxford since I was younger than Lady Rosalie is now and I can't tell you what fine, good people they are—the very cream of the aristocracy. His lordship, poor gentleman, has suffered enough in the service of his country, and he dotes on his pretty young daughter—I think it might kill him to find out what she's really like. And her ladyship who has always been so good to me—I couldn't bear to think of the scandal, her being a lady-in-waiting to the Queen, which of course she'd have to resign from. And poor young Lord Swaine in the Guards, the heir to the earldom—would he ever live down the disgrace of it? It was all too horrid to imagine. So I told Lady Rosalie to leave it to me, I'd pay off Alice and make her understand it was all she'd ever get—but only if the pair of them gave me a solemn oath they'd say goodbye to each other for good and all." Bitterly, "I might have guessed what a promise from those two would be worth!"

Distant cheering reached them from Constitution Hill.

"I knew exactly what I had to do," she continued, "and how I was going to do it. I wrote Alice a letter saying I had the money she was demanding, only I didn't intend to be seen in her company, so I'd put it between the pages of a certain book in the Old Library and she could get it from there any time after seven-thirty last Tuesday evening. She was to leave the rest of those letters in its place—I knew of course she'd never do that, only it wasn't going to matter. But I did leave the money where I said just in case something happened to stop me doing what I'd planned."

"Excuse me," Harry said, "Would you tell me the title of the book you were using?"

She gave him a surprised look. "Does it matter? It was Volume Three of *The Life and Campaigns of Napoleon Bonaparte.*"

NAPOLEON.

"Thank you. I'm sorry to interrupt."

"My father was a policeman and after he died I took his truncheon and kept it always with me. Her ladyship has some valuable jewellery and I thought one day it might come in useful. I suppose you might say in the end it did. I had it hidden inside my dress when I went to the Old Library. I hid myself behind a curtain hoping nobody else would come in and start reading, but I needn't have worried, I hadn't been there ten minutes when she arrived.

"And then everything nearly went wrong, because that disgusting old Lord Wittlesham followed her in and tried to interfere with her. I daresay any other time she'd have been willing enough, being the sort she was, but she was too eager to get her claws on that money, so she soon sent him packing.

"She found the book where I'd told her to look for it. She opened it and took the money out, then she took two letters out of her pocket to put in the book. I stepped out and hit her over the head as hard as I could before she properly realized I was there.

"I'd hoped I'd only have to hit her once, then I was going to try and arrange things so it'd look as if she'd fallen off the ladder they keep in there. But when she was on the floor I saw she was still moving, so I had to hit her again and then again—I don't know how many times. After that I knew there was no sense in trying to make it look like an accident.

"I took back the money and the two letters, then with the

truncheon hidden under my dress again I went to my room and changed all my clothes. There was blood on them that I washed off later. I'd found out where Alice's room was and I went there after making sure the girl who shared it with her was still in the servants' hall. There was a locked trunk under the bed and I had a bit of a search for the key to it. She hadn't had it on her so I knew it must be there somewhere. I found it in the pocket of her coat. I opened the trunk. The little devil had been keeping three more of those letters back. I took them out and put everything back as I'd found it. Later on I tore up all five letters and flushed them piece by piece down the toilet.

"That's all I have to tell you. As I said, I don't have any regrets. I did what I considered my duty. If I were to live this last week over again I wouldn't act any different."

The cheers from Constitution Hill were growing in volume. She said, "They'll be here in a minute. I should like to go upstairs and see them pass." And as he hesitated, "I won't be joining the others, I shall go to my own bedroom on the top floor." She met his eyes and held them while seconds passed, then with a slight shrug he turned his head and she moved quickly and quietly out of the door. Outside the cheering rose to its climax, drowning the voice from the loudspeaker till a minute or so had passed.

And in the sixth carriage the Maharajah of Chukapura and Sir Wilfred Jennings, Master of the King's Household, with two Ladies-in-Waiting to the Queen: the Marchioness of Wittlesham and the Countess of Ruxford.

They were still cheering, but not loudly enough now to cover the dread sound that was to haunt Harry Bennett through the rest of his life.

26

From *The Times* — Tuesday, 7 May 1935:

JUBILEE DAY TRAGEDY

A woman fell to her death from a window in Grosvenor Place while watching yesterday's procession. Lucy Grant, 29, was lady's maid to the Countess of Ruxford, a Lady-in-Waiting to the Queen, who was riding in a carriage of the Royal Procession. Miss Grant was alone in her bedroom on the third floor of the Earl of Ruxford's London house. Police have appealed for witnesses to come forward but are of the opinion that the tragedy was caused by the victim's eagerness to miss none of the passing pageantry.

Extract from Harry Bennett's record:

I admit frankly that I was under no illusion as to her intention. Ought I to have held her back? As a conscientious police officer I would not have hesitated had the circumstances been normal; but this was a case to which none of the accepted standards of police conduct could be applied.

Had I saved Lucy Grant from herself I am sure I would also have been saving her for the hangman, by which time the scandal she gave her life to avert would have been out and her sacrifice would have been in vain. I acted according to her wish—and, like her, I should act no differently were I able to live that week over again.

The application of logic however does little to lessen my sense of guilt. My conduct has been endorsed by those few persons in possession of the facts behind it, but I fear I shall never be able to look back on the climax of that unpublicized case without self-reproach.

Were I a religious man I should no doubt try to relieve my conscience in the confessional. To me, no regular churchgoer, that would be hypocrisy; therefore I must content myself with committing all to paper in the hope that my behaviour on that long-ago Jubilee Day will be understood and condoned by those who may read this record when I am gone and the need for secrecy no longer exists.